MYSTERIUM I
ROME

Second Edition

MITCHEL FIDEL

ISBN-13: 978-1-946469-02-1

Sheltering Tree . Earth, LLC Publishing
PO Box 973, Eagle Lake, FL 33839

ShelteringTree.Earth/writer-guidelines

About the Cover Design: The fragment of parchment is an opening page
of a fourth-century copy of the *Book of Matthew*. At the bottom appear the
Greek words **EVANGELION KATA MAT.** The portrait of *Jesus as The
Good Shepherd* reflects the earliest known manner in which Jesus was
depicted in art, sometime in the first century.
~ Mitchel Fidel

DEDICATION

To all seekers
"Seek and you shall find."
"Quaerite et invenietis"
"Zeteite kai euresete"

CONTENTS

Foreword to Second Edition   i

I   Perusing the Library   1

II   Enjoying the Home   24

III   Relishing the Goddess   35

IV   Abhorring the Gore   40

V   Inspecting the Treasure   45

VI   Meeting the Beast   51

VII   Visiting the Catacombs   68

VIII   Deriding the Apostle   78

IX   Interviewing the Patrician   83

X   Securing the Scroll   98

XI   Beholding the God   105

XII   Consulting the Archive   115

XIII   Winnowing the Details   119

XIV   Enjoying the Graces   127

XV   Befriending the Prince   134

XVI   Beginning the Journey   140

🏛   Glossary   144

Bibliography   151

About the Author   154

Discussion Guide   155

FOREWORD

Unsurprisingly, the premise of **Mysterium I Rome** has aroused a great deal of interest. That premise is the decision of a young Roman scholar in the year 100 AD to seek out the last surviving eyewitnesses to the life of Jesus in order to ascertain the truth behind that life of unparalleled significance. **Mysterium I Rome** is the first novel in a pentalogy of novels that will lead our hero, Theophilus, to four other Mysterium settings: Greece, Asia, Judea and Egypt. Within this sequence, there await for Theophilus ever more mysterious lands and ever deeper aspects of the Grand Secret that exceeds all other secrets, known in ancient times as the Mysterium.

It must be admitted, Theophilus himself is somewhat spoiled, somewhat green, and somewhat full of himself. He is, all in all, somewhat in need of a deepening. And the unique quest upon which he embarks in volume one of the pentalogy provides exactly that. Though not exactly a standout personality himself, he serves as a sounding board for some of the most fascinating greats and near-greats of ancient times: Tacitus, Pliny, Clement of Rome (alias Pope Clement), and even Emperor Trajan and Emperor Hadrian, the last character being, it so happens, the most powerful human being on earth until the Industrial Revolution. Moreover, there ring out the distant voices of Paul (Theophilus meets his attorney) and the gospel-writers, as part of the evidentiary trail in this nonpareil detective novel. And despite this book's insistence, on the cover, that important ancient wisdom resides in ancient scrolls, Theophilus's adventures are not all scholarly ones. He is driven not only by youthful vigorous curiosity, but also by youthful vigorous lust. These two drives converge in such unusual and uproarious scenarios as Theophilus's torrid affair with an actual daughter of the man who was regarded as the *Beast* of the Bible.

Our protagonist's peregrinations are highly picaresque, in an age that was far more picaresque than the age in which that rollicking word was invented. Ancient Rome was raw, raw, raw. And it was raucous. And it was colorful to a rather mad degree. Theophilus, a Roman, carries that particular setting with him into settings that become ever more exotic as he trudges down Roman road after Roman road. Such is his ever stranger yet ever more fruitful quest for the real Jesus. And one might well say that that matters, because Jesus stands out as the single most important personage at the base of our western culture.

Does the second edition of **Mysterium I Rome** not tempt? Readers have found much to criticize in **Mysterium I Rome**, *first edition*, but that is certainly not a symptom of a dull adventure. Readers have also found much to debate, much to research further, much to learn and digest and appreciate, and also much reason to look forward to the other four volumes in this one-of-kind series.

I PERUSING THE LIBRARY

In all of wonder-filled Rome, thought Theophilus, there was no more magnificent sight. Yellow-brown papyrus scrolls lay row upon row in the half-light, filling shelf after shelf, piled high along musty corridors: a catacomb of ideas waiting to be revealed at a touch. Theophilus followed an attendant through the library cellar, delighted to run his fingers along the abundance of manuscripts, eager to bring to life just one, eager to discover and unroll the scroll that would unravel a mystery.

The close of the first century A.D. was only a few months away, but that calculation could mean nothing to Theophilus. Oblivious to that particular arbitrary detail, he was reflecting on how Roman and Greek history stretched back some eight centuries or more, and how, although any individual papyrus scroll could be expected to last barely a century or two, these thousands of volumes exuded an ancientness that entailed far more than merely their mildewed smell.

From each scroll hung a *titulus*, a tag bearing the title and author. Men long dead begged the passerby's attention, calling out, "Choose me!" from a titulus. All these men had long made, and would continue to make, a bid for immortality. Theophilus scrutinized a titulus and smiled, wondering how enduring would be the immortality of the author of *Changes in the Names of Fish*.

The attendant stopped, bent forward, blinked, and peered at a pile of papyrus. He had found the book that Theophilus had requested. He removed it, but not without some difficulty, as it was a double volume, two scrolls which were both of about the maximum feasible length. Each scroll would measure some thirty-five feet if fully unrolled. That was quite a lot of expensive papyrus. Moreover, Theophilus could see that this was a deluxe edition. The scroll's roller-sticks were of ivory and the scrolls were housed in fine purple leather. And why not? This was the best library in Rome.

This library, Emperor Augustus' gift to the city a century ago, sat on the same prestigious site as the emperor's own palace: the venerable Palatine Hill overlooking the Forum. A temple of Apollo within a colonnade divided the library into halves, one for Latin books and one for Greek. Theophilus had made his inquiry in the Greek section, and the attendant now led him to its reading room.

Augustus, said to have found Rome a city of brick and left it a city of marble, had not skimped on marble here. The enormous reading room glittered with marble of every color. A not unpleasant murmur echoed perpetually off the marble, for hundreds of men sat at their scrolls, softly enunciating melodious Greek phrases to themselves. Rare was the man who had mastered the art of reading silently. That skill was difficult, as punctuation and spaces between words were practically unknown. Every text was a daunting mass of run-on capital letters without relief... *scriptuo continua*. Theophilus was a library enthusiast who was well prepared to deal with this din. Like many others here he would stuff his ears with wax. It was a droll situation, everyone admitted. Once Theophilus had composed a poem comparing a library reading room to Odysseus' ship at the island of the Sirens, and the poem had been gratifyingly well received by library connoisseurs.

But now to unravel the volumes and the mystery, thought

Theophilus. The attendant was re-rolling the scrolls on the reading table at which Theophilus sat. Extremely rare was the reader who ever bothered to perform this tedious chore for his successor. This librarian had been especially helpful all along, chattering amiably, explaining the intricate cataloguing system, and even letting Theophilus wander among the shelves with him. He had received a generous tip, of course, but something else might lie behind his attitude. The books that Theophilus was about to read were somewhat controversial. So Theophilus wondered. Could this librarian be a Christian, or an informer, or some other form of potential pest?

At last, the mammoth rolls were ready. The attendant was thanked. The wax plugs were stuffed into place. With deepest appreciation Theophilus rubbed the deluxe volume's top quality papyrus, smoothed with pumice, and breathed in the cedar-oil fragrance. Then he looked to make sure that the title on the papyrus matched the one on the titulus, which was by no means always the case. The two volumes read, *The Good News of Our Lord Jesus Christ* and *The Acts of the Apostles*. Both were by someone called Luke the Physician. Theophilus began with the first volume, the one that promised good news. The opening read:

> Many have undertaken to compile a narrative of the things seen among us, following traditions handed down to us by those who from the beginning were eyewitnesses and ministers of the word, and I, who have painstakingly gone over all these matters myself, deemed it timely to write an orderly narrative for you, most excellent Theophilus, that you may know the truth concerning the things of which you have been informed.

There it was: a perfectly standard dedication for a work in Greek. Theophilus had sought out this book for the very reason that he had heard that it was dedicated to someone named Theophilus. But no one knew who that Theophilus was. The inspiration for giving infant Theophilus his name had originated here, or so he had heard. He had hardly known his father, and his mother not at all. But a family friend had claimed that the name Theophilus derived from this book. And someone else had said that a copy could be found in this library. Theophilus touched the lone mention of his name. Who was this Theophilus? Had his parents known this Theophilus? And the thought arose that was a little unsettling: had his parents been Christians?

Theophilus proceeded with the text. "In the days of Herod, king of Judea..." Suddenly he noticed that an elderly gentleman was hovering beside him. The man acted unabashedly curious to see what Theophilus was reading; this was an activity that was just barely acceptable in the etiquette of libraries. The man's age helped to make it more acceptable. He looked pleased to see the "Luke" text, and gave a little grin and a nod which Theophilus politely returned. He wondered what it was that interested the stranger. Christianity? Fine books? Fine young men? He looked down to concentrate on his hand-span-wide columns of finely hand-lettered Greek.

"In the days of Herod, king of Judea..." This text had a fairy tale quality. The narrative concerned a number of devout Jewish people who were visited by angels who announced the impending birth of a savior... "In those days a decree went out from Caesar Augustus that all the world should be enrolled..." The parents-to-be of the Jewish savior, Joseph and Mary, needed to travel from their home in Galilee to the town of Bethlehem because of Augustus' decree concerning a census. The local inn had no room for them, and the infant Jesus was born in a barn and placed in a manger.

And then, back came the angels! They appeared to a group of shepherds to inform them that the baby who had been placed in the manger was a savior, Christ the Lord. Theophilus looked up. Now the elderly gentleman was back again. Why in heaven's name was he hovering about again? He seemed himself almost like an angel trying to break into the story, so cloudy white was he: all white-haired and white-pale and white of robe and tunic, and so beneficent-looking as he smiled down upon the unfolding narrative. Theophilus sighed and hoped that at least this man was not one of those fanciers of young men who tended to hang about the public baths. Theophilus was a handsome young man and those characters could become rather tiresome.

Theophilus read on. Jesus astounded his teachers with his knowledge of Holy Scripture at the age of twelve. Then the narrative skipped ahead to Jesus' thirtieth year, when he began his ministry "in the fifteenth year of the reign of Tiberius Caesar." That placed a definite date on what was being related: it had occurred seventy years ago.

Theophilus' mind periodically wandered from the text to wonder what the elderly gentleman was doing. Theophilus could see that the man was busily collecting material from all over the library and enlisting the librarians' assistance in his endeavors. The fellow certainly seemed to know his way around the library. And he looked much too refined to be a simple pest.

More and more, Theophilus found himself looking away from the book, which had its dull stretches, to see what the stranger was doing. The book's lowest point was reached with a dreary genealogy of Jesus. Luke's Greek was excellent, but his storytelling seemed uneven and rather pointless. Then, with Jesus' actual ministry, the pace began to pick up. Jesus resisted the temptations of the devil, telling him, "Man does not live by bread alone." He recruited some fishermen as disciples, telling them he would make them fishers of men, and recruited a despised tax collector, explaining, "Those who are well have no need of a physician, but those who are sick." Jesus was coming alive as a character. Theophilus liked his sayings: "Blessed are you that weep now, for you shall laugh"... "To him who strikes you on the cheek offer the other also"... "Forgive and you will be forgiven, give and it will be given to you"... "As you wish that men would do to you, so do to them."

Theophilus became engrossed in the Jesus story, and by the time he thought to look around again for the elderly gentleman, the left-hand roll, the finished portion of the Book of Luke, was as thick as the unfinished right. Theophilus was much impressed with Jesus' parables, and his favorite one involved a "good Samaritan" who aided a man in distress when all others scorned to do so. But not until the parable of the prodigal son did the old gentleman reappear, still busying himself with whatever research it was that had caught his fancy.

Jesus battled unsavory-seeming men called Pharisees and other forces of darkness. Theophilus commended Luke for writing a drama whose outcome he was becoming eager to see. No less intriguing was this white-haired stranger's own little drama. He now had quite a little pile of wax tablets and pottery shards on which were etched his notes. He arranged his little treasure lovingly. "Sell all that you have and distribute to the poor and you will have treasure in heaven," Theophilus read, and had to smile. Luke seemed to have an obsession with money. One incident after another concerned money. Theophilus imagined a very poor but well-educated man hunched over a rough, ill-lit table, brightening his days in some miserable hovel by scratching out this epic.

Theophilus was not the least disappointed in the epic's climax and denouement. The pathos of a last supper, a betrayal, an arrest and a trial were followed by the only details of Jesus' life that Theophilus was already familiar with: crucifixion and a rising from the grave.

"Well done," pronounced Theophilus silently. From the depths of tragedy to a turnaround in the happiest of happy endings. Wishing to rest his eyes for a minute, he began rerolling the scroll.

"Something of a minor classic, don't you think?" The elderly gentleman's voice was ghostly through the earplugs even though he was right beside Theophilus. The fellow was smiling gently and Theophilus returned the smile.

"With reservations. Yes, with some reservations I suppose you could well say that."

"To me it's written in an excellent Greek as well," opined the gentleman. "From Asia Minor, I'd say. To my mind Asia Minor is really quite underrated as regards literature. Well, you'll be wanting to read the second volume now. When you're done you might be interested in something I have here to show you. I'll be in the garden if you'd care to see it."

"Certainly, I'll be glad to take a look." Theophilus' smile was most genuine. He was looking forward to the stranger's surprise, since he had all the appearances of a man who was full of information.

"Excellent!" declared the stranger. " Oh, and don't feel you have to hurry on my account."

The gentleman gathered up his notes and walked off, rather too rheumatically for an angel.

Now Theophilus took on the second huge scroll. It began with an introduction much like the first scroll's introduction. "In the first book, O Theophilus, I have dealt with all that Jesus began to do and teach until the day when he was taken up." Luke went on to describe how Jesus descended from heaven to imbue the apostles with magical powers, all except the traitor Judas who "bought a field with the reward of his wickedness and falling headlong he burst open in the middle and all his bowels gushed out."

This passage about Judas's guts spilling out typified the *Book of Acts* for Theophilus. It often seemed to him a great conglomeration of silliness. He was appalled when the Spirit of the Lord struck a husband and wife dead for having secretly withheld a portion when they donated all of their possessions to the apostles. This seemed like an all-too-obvious literary ploy to ensure funding for a cult through scare tactics. The apostles made tiresome speeches and worked miracles that were palpably less interesting than those of Jesus; and Theophilus believed Jesus' miracles to have been the least edifying aspect of his biography anyway.

The *Book of Acts* story was more to Theophilus' taste when a man named Paul made his entry. Paul persecuted the Christians, ferociously, guarding the garments of a mob while the mob stoned a prominent Christian to death, Stephen by name. Then, suddenly one day while he was on the road to Damascus, a blinding light from heaven knocked Paul to the ground and Jesus himself appeared to him. From then on Paul was the most determined of Christian missionaries, a spicy dramatic turnaround. Paul's missionary activity was described in great detail, while the original apostles receded into the background, even Peter the chief one. Once it was formally decided that the apostles would preach to Jews and Paul would preach to non-Jews, Acts concerned almost exclusively the acts of Paul.

Theophilus rubbed his eyes. These were long books, certainly more than enough for an afternoon's reading. The Jesus story, the *Gospel of Luke*, had been an entertaining fable. As for the sequel, the Book of Acts, Theophilus frankly could not imagine why anyone had written it. At one point Luke seemed to be intimating that he himself was traveling with Paul, but he gave no details about himself whatsoever. Paul's adventures continued: beatings, riots, debates, arrests, and even a shipwreck. All seemed to be building to a resolution that would occur at Paul's long-awaited trial in Rome. Then, much to Theophilus' surprise, the narrative cut off abruptly with the flattest of endings while Paul still sat waiting in prison, "teaching about the Lord Jesus Christ quite openly and unhindered."

Theophilus wavered between feeling cheated and feeling relieved that the epic was over. In truth, it had been more than enough reading for one afternoon. He sent the two Luke scrolls back to the cellar with a librarian and walked to the garden.

There sat the old gentleman, straining to read a scroll in inadequate sunlight, oblivious to various hand-whirling conversations that swirled around him here and there. This was a pathetic sight, this the eventual fate of most literary aficionados: failing eyes coupled with too much pride to hire a reader.

"Ah, hello young man! Come sit over here with me!" The gentleman's eyesight was not so hopeless after all. "I'm too old to bother impressing people with my ponderous string of three names. Nowadays I like to be called simply Cato."

Theophilus sat on the pink marble bench beside Cato. "And I'm Theophilus."

Cato raised a white eyebrow. "Theophilus? That's your name? Quite a coincidence! Or is it a coincidence?"

"Actually, it isn't at all. I was very young when my father died. Only recently, it so happened, I began to wonder why he named me Theophilus."

"Was your father a Christian?"

"That's one of the things I hope to find out. Anyway, not long ago I found out about my name's being mentioned in the introductions of those Luke books, and I learned that there were copies of both of them in this library."

"Yes. It's not something that would have been allowed here a few years ago." For a few moments Cato had that distant look that Theophilus had often noticed on older Romans as they recalled one sampling or another of *the bad old days*. "But it's high-quality literature, after all. They couldn't deny it admission forever. You've studied in Greece, I assume?"

"Many, many years. I probably know Greece better than Italy. I was a young orphan, a wealthy young orphan, and sending me off to study in Greece was the obvious thing to do with me."

"Greece is a second home to me as well," reminisced Cato. "I was both a student and a teacher of law and philosophy there. However, I spent most of my life as a magistrate right here in Rome. Now that I'm retired, here I am back here in 'little Greece' almost every day. I suppose I'm as much a part of the library as is the furniture. You seem to have some degree of leisure yourself."

"I own an estate in Venetia. Living there holds no real interest for me. So I decided to try living in Rome, and my first concern here was these two Luke books and satisfying my curiosity about my name. Can you tell me anything about this other Theophilus who Luke knew?"

"Theophilus, Theophilus, a good name, Theophilus. A good philosopher's name: The Lover of God. But I'm afraid you're not going to be finding any other Theophilus, Theophilus. You see, what I'm sure that Luke was doing, by dedicating his work to a Theophilus, was dedicating his work to 'The Lover of God' in general."

"I see. And what can you tell me about Luke himself?"

"Whoever Luke the Physician may have been, I can almost guarantee you one thing: he was not really named Luke the Physician! Luke the Physician is a very fitting pseudonym that means The Healing Light. So, you see now, in the two Luke volumes the Jesus story is presented by The Healing Light to any Lover of God. You see, what the author set out to do, as he stated in the introduction, was to supersede all the other Jesus biographies and make the story available to a more cultured class of people than had previously been the case. And, indeed, Luke's *Jesus story* is the only one good enough to be honored with acceptance in this library. And in deluxe editions, no less."

Theophilus stroked his chin and nodded. Cato was one welcome fixture in the library as far as he was concerned. "So, there are other Jesus stories?" he asked.

"There are something like eighty, but I've seen nowhere near that many of them myself. And I do try! I study the eastern superstitions as a hobby, you see."

"Then I'm curious to know what you've concluded. All the superstitious nonsense and miracles aside, this Jesus must have been a great teacher, a brave martyr."

"Now who are you really describing?" Cato replied with a question of his own. "You and I are steeped in Greek culture. To us there can be no greater man than Socrates. We want Jesus to be Socrates. But everything looks quite different to an oriental mind."

"Certainly. Certainly Jesus' story has been embellished,

perhaps almost beyond recognition. What the average Roman knows about the man certainly isn't worth a bronze penny, and that's very likely true about the average Christian as well. Have you ever spoken to anyone who actually knew Jesus?"

Cato shook his head. "No. No, I haven't, unfortunately. And by now it's probably too late."

"Why? Seventy years' time admittedly makes it difficult to find witnesses to a man's life, but not impossible. It wouldn't be impossible to talk to witnesses, and, really, someone should do exactly that before it's too late!"

"I quite agree. But since you've become interested in Jesus let me show you the notes I just compiled."

Theophilus was deep in thought. The words he had just spoken were echoing in his head, and it was some time before he noticed that Cato was expounding on the very surprise that he had recently been so eager to see.

"Here's what I figured would shed new light on the Luke books for you," explained Cato as he spread his wax tablets and pottery shards out on their bench. "When I was a lad, old men always spoke of this with awe: the way Emperor Augustus ended decades of agonizing worldwide strife and established the Pax Romana, the *Roman Peace*. Well, you know your history, no doubt. You know that this was a feat never paralleled. So look at what we have here in the old literature.

"See here in the old writings: Augustus described as the Prince of Peace, the Son of God, the bringer of a new golden age and a new generation. Virgil here goes on and on about Augustus as a savior and a redeemer. The sources are endless. They composed a veritable propaganda flood! Here's a description of how Augustus' mother Atia dreamed, during a visit to a temple of Apollo, that the god impregnated her by means of a snake. It seems somewhat reminiscent of what's called the Annunciation, the announcement that Mary would bear the son of God.

"Virgil wrote a prophecy that a divine savior would arrive by means of a virgin birth, and here with Atia giving birth to Augustus was the prophecy's fulfillment. Here's a description of a shower of falling stars that prompted Augustus to order twelve-day advent celebrations to welcome the coming of the millennium; that's reminiscent of the star that announced Jesus' birth. And here you see how Augustus drove out demons and cleansed the temples. And there's this snippet about Augustus: 'The birthday of God has brought to the world glad tidings… From his birthday a new era begins.' I think the implications are clear."

"A broad borrowing of literary motifs."

"More than just that. If you know anything about the Jews you know that among them the notion of Augustus as a redeemer had to be rejected utterly. The Jews wanted their own redeemer! I believe that these literary motifs, as you call them, were circulating among the Jews when Jesus died a martyr, and the Augustus motifs immediately attached themselves to Jesus."

"One would think that rising from the dead would have been the only trick Jesus would need," commented Theophilus.

"That and raising all others from the dead would certainly be the feat that no other redeemer could surpass. I'm not prepared to believe that Jesus did that. Yet he must have done something. Thousands have been willing to go to the lions or the sword happily praising his name. This alleged wonderworker indubitably worked that one particular wonder at least. I've seen people making themselves martyrs to emulate the martyr. But I'm afraid we'll never know for certain what else he may have done."

"That's not true at all!" objected Theophilus. "There must be witnesses still alive in Judea, or at least people who've talked to witnesses!"

"There have been wars, persecutions, mass expulsions of Jews. Jerusalem is a pile of ruins. I wish the investigator a great deal of luck!"

"Wish me luck then! I intend to be that investigator!" Theophilus was surprised to hear himself blurt out the words.

People were looking at Theophilus. He realized he had been rather loud for the past few minutes. Suddenly someone sneezed.

"By Jupiter!" exclaimed Cato. "Who could ask for a more perfect omen? The gentleman who just sneezed is sitting to your right, Theophilus! The success of your ventured is assured!"

"At least I'll guarantee you it wasn't intentional!" declared the stout, bald man who had sneezed. "To invoke superstition to bless someone's quest to write about superstition! I'd say it's a lot of folly! Don't get it into your head to write about the Christians, young man. There's danger there."

"Utter nonsense!" countered another man seated nearby. "Those days died with Domitian."

"That's right," agreed Cato. "Anyway, if ever one is suspected of being a Christian a pinch of incense sacrificed to a statue of the emperor has always sufficed to get one off the hook."

"Still and all," said the man who had sneezed, "this remains a dangerous world and I wouldn't advise anyone to be identified in any way shape or form with the Christians."

He was contradicted by the man who had contradicted him before. "Come now, this lad merely wants to find out the truth. If some author essays to write about whether Cyclopes ever really existed does that make the author a Cyclops? Of course not. I think this lad has a fine idea. For as long as I can remember everybody has been predicting that the Christians would soon disappear, but they haven't. Whatever this Christ person stood for, for good or evil, we should find out the truth about him. And as the lad pointed out it may soon be too late!"

"Son, listen to me," urged the sneezer, putting a friendly hand on Theophilus' shoulder. "I have just one word to say to you... Mithraism." There arose a murmur of protest, which, the sneezer endeavored to overrule loudly. "Mithraism is the up-and-coming superstition! The Christians keep predicting the end of the world! What's going to happen to them when the world doesn't end, hmm? Then you're really stuck, I'd say! Then who's going to have any interest in the book you worked so hard on, hmm?"

"I for one!" chimed in the sneezer's antagonist, now placing a rival friendly hand on Theophilus' shoulder. "Young man, when you finish your book bring it to me and I'll make you an extra copy or two in exchange for the right to make a copy for myself."

Theophilus smiled. This friendly fellow did not realize how little Theophilus needed his offer. This was a standard offer: one of the means by which starving authors could earn some silver in the complete absence of royalties or copyright, or even printing.

Cato explained. "Gentlemen, young Theophilus here is a man of means! He has money and leisure, and for a man in such a position I can think of no more honorable occupation than the writing of an important book! And when he's done, he has the means to order up fifty copies or more! He can inundate the Empire with them! I'd say we're witnessing a historic occasion!"

The ring of observers seemed to approve. More importantly, a second ring of observers seemed to approve, for the garden was surrounded by the busts of great authors of the past. Hardly a man present would have hesitated to give up everything to be among those busts. For a few moments all were silent. They were reverent members of a holy fellowship. Then the garrulous sneezer chose to speak up again.

Soon he and his opponent were at their old game once more. And their debate spilled over and stirred up ripples and eddies of other debates in ever-expanding circles. Theophilus smiled even more broadly than before, showing fine teeth that would be the envy of most of these older men. Italy could never be boring, he said to himself. A few words on any subject at all would set the Italians off, with hands gesticulating, shoulders shrugging, eyes bulging, and fingertips clasping upward into finely shaken delicate points to make finely elucidated rhetorical points.

Cato sighed. "Lord of Olympus, my boy, with only a few words you've managed to fire up more enthusiasm than I've seen here in a very long time! If your book turns out to be anything like this..." He shrugged helplessly. "Now you really have to do as you said: go to Judea and find Jesus Christ!"

"I fully intend to do so! A project like this is exactly what I've been needing!"

"I rather envy you the blazing of a whole new path in literature. Non-Christian literature I mean. You know, that's one of the odd things about Jesus. You'd expect that he'd have made some impact on the Judea of his day, but any mention of him is entirely missing in the authors who you'd expect to have mentioned him: Philo, Josephus, Justus of Tiberias, Pliny."

Offered Theophilus, "Well, Philo was a philosopher rather than a historian. And Josephus? A turncoat and an opportunist. He'd write only what suited him. I don't know much about Justus of Tiberias. As for Pliny, well, he put so much into his encyclopedia that you can hardly fault him for the enormous amount that he left out. Or for what he misunderstood completely."

"No. I can't hear that said about Pliny. Not Pliny." Cato looked offended. He wore an unpleasant expression on his face for the first time since Theophilus had seen him. Theophilus had apparently found and upset a true Pliny devotee. Many scholars virtually idolized Pliny and his encyclopedia.

This time the sneezer's intervention was timely. "Say, just in case you really want to get into a hot discussion about that, did you know that Pliny's nephew Pliny the Younger is actually here today? He's with Cornelius Tacitus. Say, as a matter-of-fact Tacitus is just the one to set you straight about Mithraism, isn't he? Why don't I see if I can find them?"

The sneezer's opponent addressed Theophilus as the sneezer left the garden. "They say Pliny had the stamina of Hercules. He's supposed to have consulted two thousand works in order to compile his encyclopedia. Are you prepared to do the same for your book?"

"I'll have plenty of time to consult two thousand works after I've interviewed witnesses and people who have talked to witnesses," replied Theophilus. "They come first."

"But you've got all winter to get a grounding in the appropriate literature," suggested Cato. "I'll be glad to help you get started."

"Thank you. You're right. I can't travel during the winter, of course. But there should be plenty that I can find out right here in Rome. How about this Paul, for instance? Luke left him sitting in prison in Rome. Do you know what happened to him?"

"Indeed, I do." Cato sounded rather proud of the fact. "It's a line of inquiry I've looked into. So, I can introduce you to someone who knew Paul. I'll have you talk to the very man who was the assistant to the counselor assigned by the state to Paul's case. Paul was extremely important, you know. Everyone has heard of the Twelve Apostles. It was Luke who popularized the idea of Twelve Apostles, the twelve main followers of Jesus. The term 'apostle' originally meant someone who had seen the risen Christ. But Paul, who never saw the living Christ, claimed to have seen the risen Christ, or some reasonable facsimile thereof. So some see Paul as the greatest of the apostles. Luke thought highly of the notion of Twelve Apostles, but in his *Book of Acts* nine of the Twelve Apostles have absolutely nothing to do! The book is almost all about Paul! Yes, Paul was of the utmost importance. I'll have you talk to my friend who knew Paul."

"Excellent! Now what about this Pontius Pilate? He must have been known in Rome."

Cato folded his hands and looked down. Then he proceeded to speak more like the lawyer he was. "The Christians first came to people's attention when Nero chose them as a scapegoat to divert the suspicion that he himself had started the Great Fire in order to have a cleared Rome for his building schemes. Hundreds of Christians were roasted alive on crosses up on the Vatican. You know how ill-omened is the Vatican, named as it is because it has always been a favorite haunt of witches, *vates*. So Nero had Christians roasted alive on the Vatican, and had others torn apart by attack dogs. Nero had the Christians executed on the Vatican partly because it was a place of such ill repute and partly because it was near his circus. I myself saw him riding around the Vatican in a chariot enjoying the show.

"It was a night that those of my generation will never forget, the night of the human torches. From most of the city you could see them burn, up on the Vatican bluffs across the Tiber. Anyway, it was on that night that many people started asking who this Jesus, called the Christ, had been, and before long everybody was asking about Pontius Pilate. There were still some alive who had known him."

All leaned forward to hear what would come next. But the nature of the "Fire of Rome" story caused Cato to delay his narrative as he reached for a jug of wine and a cup. He gulped greedily before continuing.

"As you can tell from the name Pilate, 'Spear-carrier,' this character was from a professional military family; he wasn't a well-bred sort at all. I'll tell you what Philo had to say about Pilate: 'Naturally inflexible, a blend of self-will and relentlessness, a man noted for vindictiveness and a furious temper.' He was exactly the sort of uncouth oaf that tended to reach high office during the rule of that dreadful cur Sejanus. While Emperor Tiberius hid from the world on Capri, his deputy Sejanus did whatever he liked, appointing all sorts of lower-class adventurers like himself. Naturally, Pilate was a disaster when ruling Judea. There was disturbance after disturbance, which I'm sure could have been avoided by a man not so completely out of his depth as Pilate.

"Pilate was forcibly retired in disgrace and lived on in Rome, childless and almost friendless. It was mostly rather distant acquaintances who gave a description of him to the curious: dour, cold, cynical, suspicious, and temperamental. Well, he was precisely like the emperor he served, wasn't he? But maybe a little different, in that he was incompetent. Plenty of such incompetents received appointments beyond their capabilities under Sejanus.

And plenty of them were executed when Sejanus fell. But I heard that Pilate was finished off during the Caligula terror. A great pity, some said, since he would have dearly enjoyed the night of the living torches."

Suddenly all eyes were on the far end of the garden. There the man who sneezed was leading in Tacitus and Pliny the Younger, both of whom were literary celebrities well known to those present, even a recent arrival like Theophilus. More than that, the pair were both dignitaries of the Empire, men of senatorial rank who were well on their way up the "course of honors" ladder of successive governmental offices, and as such they merited a somewhat hushed scene of entrance.

To Theophilus, they seemed to exude power in two very different ways. Pliny, the larger and handsomer of the two, stepped confidently into each new position that he occupied in his world, radiating good will and good sense. Tacitus had the look of a censor, with eyes darting about ferret-like in a homely bald skull, eyes ever seeking out objects, ideas or people unworthy of being in Rome. Around Rome some had whispered that he looked hatchet-faced, resembling a fasces. This was the axe tied up in a bundle of rods that was one of the more menacing emblems of Rome, since it symbolized the state's power to beat and execute.

Cato greeted the celebrities on behalf of the little group and introduced Theophilus.

"So you're the young fellow who wants to write about Christians!" exclaimed Tacitus in orator's tones. "I could have sworn it was going to be that shy young friend of yours," he said turning to Pliny, "that quiet fellow who's always hanging about here, the one who wants to write history. What was his name again?"

"Suetonius."

"Yes, Suetonius. I remember I took the pains to explain to him the difference between history and annals." Tacitus addressed Theophilus. "I hope you're aware of the distinction, young man.

Any compilation of events from other people's lifetimes must be termed annals. Only if you're making an inquiry into the events of your own lifetime can your work be considered a 'history,' which is Greek for an inquiry. No doubt it's high time someone did set out to make such an inquiry about the Christians. What conclusions do you intend to set out to prove?"

"None whatever," was Theophilus' reply. "I only intend to set down truthfully whatever I happen to come upon, and I'll form no opinions about Christianity till I'm done with my research."

Tacitus and Pliny exchanged a raised-eyebrows glance that seemed to Theophilus remarkably like a scrap of theatricality from a comedy, though that could not have been intentional.

"A novel approach, if nothing else!" opined Tacitus dryly.

Pliny told Theophilus, "I suppose it is feasible to delay your conclusion till the end, my friend, but of course you realize that certain things absolutely must be decided at the outset." Pliny counted on his fingers. "You'll have to decide between 'grand,' 'middle' or 'delicate' style, and choose your sentence pattern, capsulation and rhythm and quite a lot more. Have you studied rhetoric?"

"Yes. For many years in Greece." Theophilus wondered if his face betrayed his repugnance at this memory.

"Well, no doubt you learned your lessons very well," said Pliny kindly, "but now that you're in Rome you can do so much more. If you study with my own professor of rhetoric, Quintilian, you'll be studying with the greatest rhetorician since Cicero."

"Quintilian has been very ill. He's certainly not going to take on any new students." Tacitus was forceful and Theophilus was glad. He hoped never to come near another professor of rhetoric as long as he lived, even if the man were a second Cicero."

"Oh, the old gentleman is quite fond of me," said Pliny. "I'm sure I can persuade him to take on one more student."

A major favor from a high official was being promised, a favor which Theophilus was desperate to forestall. His loathing of the idea of any more lessons in rhetoric was profound enough to make him tell two lies.

"I'm very grateful for the offer, but I'm going to Judea as soon as possible to begin my research."

"But not so terribly soon! You'll be here all winter doing preliminary research!"

Theophilus felt Cato was being most unhelpful, but also felt he meant well.

"Do you really want to go to that miserable Judea?" asked Tacitus. "You'll get no straight story out of the Jews anyway. A repulsive religion and a perverse culture is what they've got. I'll grant we're obligated to tolerate their religion, unlike Christianity, on account of its antiquity. But really, young fellow, why not do all your research right here? All you'll ever need is right here in this library."

"I admire the lad's attitude!" Theophilus' heartbeat quickened at these words of the great Pliny the Younger. "He reminds me of my Uncle Pliny. Uncle Pliny didn't just rely on what someone had said. He'd go take a look for himself! But remember, uh, Theophilus is it? Remember there's always danger lurking if you get too close to your subject. Uncle Pliny wanted to see the eruption of Mount Vesuvius up close and I'm sure you know what happened. He's under the remains of the eruption forevermore!"

"And," said Tacitus, "during that selfsame eruption the younger Pliny, perhaps the wiser Pliny, was calmly reading the works of the historian Livy. So you see, Theophilus, we historians, although every bit as interesting as volcanoes, are a good deal less dangerous!"

"Both claims could be disputed," quipped Pliny. "Anyway, you'll be joining quite a remarkable fraternity as a historian, Theophilus. Livy ultimately became so famous that they say a man once came all the way from Spain to Rome merely to see him. The man managed to get a look at Livy and then went right back to Spain! Of course, that sort of thing still hasn't happened to our dear Tacitus."

"Oh?" mused Tacitus. "Don't be so sure! For all we know it may have happened hundreds of times already!"

The observation elicited some mild laughter. Theophilus liked this merry literary loiterers' fraternity. When they were at their best, each one even had a distinctive laugh, one boisterous, one dignified, one scornful, and so on. And he was pleased that the conversation had strayed far from rhetoric. He decided to keep the conversation that way by asking Tacitus a question.

"Might I ask if you have anything you can tell me about the man who unwittingly created Christianity, the prefect Pontius Pilate whom we were just discussing?"

"I'm afraid not. But let's keep our terms straight. The man was a procurator, not a *prefect*."

"But the terms are virtually interchangeable," objected Pliny.

"No. No. There are distinctions worthy of being preserved. Proconsuls and *propraetors* are able to delegate their imperium, their power to command legions, to delegates called legates if of senatorial rank and prefects if of equestrian rank. A procurator is specifically an equestrian charged with a province but no imperium , no command of legions."

"Didn't Pilate command military auxiliaries?"

"They're not legions."

Pliny turned to Theophilus. "Well, we carry on like this endlessly, as you see. It's a stimulus, all this debating. We writers are always available to each other to encourage each other's writing, and I think that's delightful." So did Theophilus.

Cato entered into the conversation for the first time. "Tacitus, you've looked into these things. Am I correct in my recollection that people scarcely thought about Christians before they were burned alive on the Vatican?"

"The night of the living torches on the Vatican? Yes, that's right. No one can ever forget that night. Before that, the Christians were indistinguishable from the other squabbling sects of Jews. I do recall hearing that the Christ superstition often had the Jews of Rome at odds with each other. And that sectarian strife was the reason behind Claudius' expelling the Jews from Rome at one point. Nobody was ever much concerned about all that. But then came Nero's scapegoating It seemed a sly move. No one liked Christians. They were antisocial, scorning attendance at the city's shows and ceremonies and declaring it all to be meaningless because the end of the world was near. And their cult had none of the legitimacy that others could claim by virtue of antiquity. But Nero's persecution was so brutal that people ended up sympathizing with the Christians. It was all too clear that they were being sacrificed not to the public good but to the rapaciousness of a tyrant."

"And no more than that need be said about Nero," commented Pliny. "But this Pontius Pilate fellow. I think that Theophilus may have here an alluring literary device in calling him the unwitting founder of Christianity."

Tacitus' disapproving ferret eyes flashed even more hotly than during his diatribe against Nero. "If it's indeed the case, then Pilate should have been crucified himself! Christ the charlatan could have died a forgotten old beggar! Instead, Pontius Pilate stuck us with a martyr and with a pernicious superstition! And here in Rome we now have to deal with it somehow! Here in Rome where all things horrible or shameful collect as though in a cesspool!"

"A cesspool you don't seem to be in a hurry to leave," chided Pliny. "Perhaps to go back and live in a hut with the Germans!"

"Come now, all the world knows that only Rome means civilization: peace, prosperity, roads, the rule of law. I studied the Germans not to become one of them, but to learn from them. They're a primitive lot, but a virile, unspoiled race. There's a lot we had better learn from them, and soon, we who've lost so many of the old Roman virtues to a flood of decadence. So, I wrote what I regard as an indispensable warning."

"And an immortal work," said Theophilus. "I'll be content if my book turns out to be a fraction as praiseworthy as your Germania."

Tacitus now spoke to Theophilus with notable sweetness, but the fasces-faced man's sweetness could not last. "I'm confident you'll produce an outstanding work, young man. And you'll be doing society a huge service in exposing this Jesus as a fraud. The impiety of these superstition-mongers positively makes my blood boil! They prey on the gullible and threaten all mankind by turning people away from established religions and trying the patience of the gods! Crucify the Christians properly, I say! With sharp pens as nails! Historians have a holy trust. They should always be present to threaten wrongdoers with perpetual disgrace, and no group has earned disgrace more than the Christians!"

Theophilus winced. Many had been the times he had been annoyed by these moralizing stoics who constantly praised the perfection of a bygone Rome that had probably never existed. Most repellant of all were the ones who preached sanctimoniously in public and behaved depravedly in private. The emperors Tiberius and Domitian were reputed to have been that way. To deflate the moralizer's little tirade, Theophilus said simply, "I really have no interest in writing about the Christians, but only about this man Jesus. And whatever I find to have been true about him, that is what I'll say, be that truth ever so different from what we might expect!"

At this the sneezer sneezed once again and looked astonished at what he had done. Once again, he was seated at Theophilus' right. This time even the unsuperstitious among the loiterers in the garden seemed stunned enough to allow themselves to be shaken by superstition, maybe just this once.

II ENJOYING THE HOME

𝒯heophilus accepted Cato's invitation to come home for supper. A wealthy Roman's urban home was bound to be of a standard pattern. To anyone viewing from the street there was nothing but four high and, perhaps purposefully, unimpressive walls which were dotted with a few tiny windows. To a guest welcomed at the front door, on the other hand, some lovely sights awaited inside a wealthy person's home. Theophilus, a guest welcomed at the front door, toured Cato's fine home with appreciation.

He entered the house through the atrium, a square foyer which was the center of household activity. A pool that held rainwater from a great hole in the roof was the centerpiece of the atrium. He looked around to take in various tasteful features: small wall shrines to household gods, murals of nature scenes, brightly painted columns, ornate benches, and carved doors that led to various small rooms. Slaves kept all of these items very clean. They were well-trained staff, unobtrusively just barely within sight, ready to be summoned. At the back of the atrium was a corridor that Theophilus knew would have the kitchen on one side and the dining room on the other. The back of the house consisted of a porticoed garden. At the back end of a wealthy Roman's property, some decoration that acted as a theme-work for the entire

24

house would be positioned so as to be visible at a great distance from the entry. In Cato's house that summative piece of art work was a statue of Apollo, the patron of the arts and learning.

Host and guest reclined in the dining room, and the unobtrusive slaves carried in the many small dishes which together composed the main meal of the day.

Theophilus made the customary compliment. "You have a truly fine home here."

"I'm comfortable enough, but of course I have no estate," smiled Cato.

"Oh, my estate is nothing special. Enough to keep me comfortable. I have relatively simple needs. I have a man that I trust take care of the place and I go where I please. I feel too young to live the life of a rural recluse."

"And how does your family feel about that?"

"Cato, I'm the owner of an estate only because everyone else in my family was at some point carried away by pestilences. I have only distant relatives left, and only one person is left who knew me as a child: the elderly slave who travels with me. A good fellow named Titus."

"The pestilences did the same to my family," said Cato. "You'll notice it's a bit quiet around here. And Rome was struck with one plague that the countryside hardly noticed, the disease that carried away what the other diseases had left; the disease named Domitian."

Theophilus had heard such bitter words before. Domitian had been Emperor for most of Theophilus' lifetime, and until very recently. Nero was the oldest generation's object of contempt, and Caligula was little more than an antiquarian memory that was almost quaint, but Domitian's depredations were still fresh in everyone's mind. Theophilus figured he should change the subject, and a glance into the adjacent room showed him how to do that.

"May I take a look at your library?"

"Of course." They entered the library. Cato took on an

expression that was genuinely loving, and even went so far as to caress several of his books, as though they were family that he was greeting "Needless to say, everything here will be at your disposal for your research. Have a look!"

As one book lover to another, Cato smiled broadly. He was surpassingly pleased to watch Theophilus rummage through his books in rapt admiration. As for Theophilus, he did not see the smile because he was engrossed in the merry task of inspecting books and deciding which ones to peek inside. He asked, "What's this round symbol that someone has drawn on many of the scrolls?"

"Oh, that's a habit I picked up, something that's current among certain book lovers. You see, it's the Greek letter chi, looking like 'X,' superimposed on the Greek letter rho, looking like 'P.' Together they make a symbol that some people like to encircle, to make it prettier. The chi-rho stands for chrestos, 'excellent.' A very fine way to mark favored passages, wouldn't you say?"

"I would indeed! I'll start marking up books that way myself!"

"And some Christians have taken up the chi-rho as a symbol for Christ, since chrestos and Christos are so close."

"Well, it sure makes sense to have an attractive symbol."

Returning to the subject of the library, Cato offered apologetically, "I have only a small sampling of what might be of interest to you, but I can find you much more. The Christians venerate four classes of book. A book enumerating various "acts of the apostles" is one class. Today you read the main example of that class. Letters written by apostles, or other great teachers, especially Paul, are another genre, called letters or epistles. Then there is the 'apocalypse' or 'revelation.' This involves God speaking directly to a chosen messenger and revealing the future and the fate of mankind and the meaning of all things. And, finally, a 'gospel,' a 'good news,' is a life of Jesus. 'Gospel' is evangelion in Greek. An evangelion was originally a public announcement of glad tidings by a government messenger. Such announcements saturated the Empire after the Battle of Actium, when Augustus was the unrivaled master of the world and unleashed a ceaseless propaganda campaign in praise of his Pax Romana. I believe the Jews of that era quite consciously adapted the term evangelion to their own purposes."

Noted Theophilus, "I see that you also have a whole section of books that are marked as having to do with the beliefs of the Jews."

"Yes. There are three types of Jewish holy book. Firstly: Histories. Secondly: Laws. Thirdly: Prophecies." Cato snickered a bit. "To me it says a lot about the Jews that they have just these three types of book. Firstly: Worry about the past. Secondly: Worry about the present. Thirdly: Worry about the future."

"Yes, it does seem to go along with the common conception of the personality of the Jews. I do believe I prefer the Roman proclivity to grab hold of life and enjoy it in the moment. Carpe diem." Theophilus was reading title after title in the library. "You have enough here to keep me busy all winter. But you said there are eighty gospels!"

"Yes indeed, and similar numbers of works in the other genres. But as in every field most of them are by dreadful writers who are given no credence at all; or else they're favored only in the east. Here in Rome the Christians use mostly a gospel by Matthew, because Matthew was one of the twelve apostles, the one who was a tax collector. To a lesser extent, the Christians use a gospel by Mark, who was supposed to have been a companion of Peter. Mark was not an eyewitness to the life of Jesus, but some believe that he did stand with Jesus at Gethsemane. Luke, who was not a witness to the life of Jesus, comes in third as a favored gospel writer. Oh! And you'll have to read all the Jews' holy books as well. I'll send you to an old Jewish scholar I know who has all you'll need. It's a shame that Josephus himself recently died. But perhaps it's just as well. He was nothing but a liar anyway. At any rate, the Jewish literature is something you absolutely must read. Everything Christianity talks about is grounded in the thought-world of the Jews."

"Are we to think of the Christians as still a Jewish sect?"

"Both sides deny that vehemently, and violently, with bodies lying in the alleys of their slums to prove it. To Jews, the Christians are upstart mythmakers who threaten the very basis of the respectability of Judaism. It's a bitter struggle, and an uneven one. If every nook and cranny of the Empire were rigorously searched we might find 500,000 Christians out of a total population of fifty million in the Empire. Fifty million adults anyway, including women and slaves. But there are at least a half million Jews."

"Are there really so many Jews? One always hears them spoken of as a defeated folk."

"I've seen the most reliable census figures. Yes: so many Jews, all over the Empire! Perhaps half a million Jews were killed in the Jewish Revolt of thirty years ago, as incredible as that may seem. Perhaps another half million became refugees. They joined the many Jews who were already living all over the Empire, and even in many places outside the Empire such as Persia and Arabia. Jews are defeated in one sense, being largely deprived of a homeland by Vespasian's mass expulsions from Judea. But there are far more of them than could ever have lived in that homeland anyway. 'Be fruitful and multiply,' their God commanded them, and they do. No other people has such strict dietary and sanitary laws. No other people has as strict a prohibition against infanticide and abortion. All these factors keep Jewish populations large and growing."

Cato, a gracious host, correctly sensed that Theophilus was still hungry, and suggested a return to their olives, honey, and grapes.

"You can detect a lot of the Christians' antipathy against Jews in Luke's books," informed Cato, spreading butter and honey on a hunk of bread. "'This people's heart has grown dull,' Luke says at the end. Luke's books are supposed to be fairly recent works, and I think they reflect the animosity of a decisive split between Christians and Jews. Look at how Luke has the Jews treat Paul! They treat Jesus even worse, of course. I think it's no accident that Luke shows Jews behaving less honorably than Samaritans, since Samaritans are the very devil to Jews. And Luke's crucifixion story was told from a very definite point of view, you know.

Theophilus felt an urge to put in, out of politeness, "I say, Cato, the conversation has taken a rather grim turn. I hang on your every word, it's all so interesting. However as a first time guest in your house I don't want to be forcing you to expound on history and theology. Perhaps we can turn to a more pleasant topic. Perhaps you can tell me something about your family."

Cato gave a tight-lipped look that spoke volumes, and threw a glance at the one silent slave that also spoke volumes. He was a lonely man in a lonely home, and said so. "My friend, this is a home that has known much tragedy. No, this is not a time when I wish to discuss my family. All of them gone. Some other time I may wish to discuss my family, but not now. One is supposed to live for one's family, no? But being all alone, I live for my studies. They are my passion! So if it's all the same to you, I'll just continue."

He did so, as soon as Theophilus nodded.

"Luke was pretty unabashedly anti-Jew and his main aim was to make Christianity look more respectable to his cultivated Greek-speaking audience that was not Jewish. So he has the Jews howl for Jesus' death and at the same time waters down Pilate's role, making Pilate nothing but an innocent dupe of the evil Jews. In Luke's gospel, Pilate even tries to palm Jesus off on King Herod of Galilee, which I can assure you from a legal standpoint is utter bosh! Then, in nowhere else but in Luke as far as I know, Jesus says 'Father forgive them for they don't know what they're doing.' A poignant enough touch, but too obviously an apologist's attempt to show that Jesus was never a threat to the Roman state.

"Over and over, Luke demonstrates that he is trying hard to make Christianity palatable to Romans. He has Jesus cure a centurion's slave, and has Peter baptize the centurion Cornelius and the man's entire household. And, for good measure, there's Peter's baptism of the wife of Herod's steward. I really wonder how much of Luke's tale consists of contentious gossip and propaganda rather than history. In particular I don't think much of Jesus' optimistic talk with a thief while on the cross, having seen myself what crucifixion is really like. Still, I'll admit that it's all just barely possible. I've had such optimistic talks with Christians myself, including some that I was just about to sentence to be crucified."

Theophilus spit out a mouthful of wine. He was being a poor guest, but his host had as much as hit him over the head with a paving stone. He was accustomed to Romans talking casually about the most atrocious cruelties, but he had never personally witnessed such cruelties, and he was quite upset to hear such a cruelly casual confession from this angelic-looking man!

"Yes... uh, you did say you were a magistrate," stammered Theophilus.

"Don't look so distraught, my all-too-short-lived friend. Christians always knew what they were getting into. I never tricked or hounded anybody or dispensed anything but equal justice under the law. If someone accused of practicing Christianity was brought before me I would ask him three times if the accusation were true, repeating each time the capital nature of the offense. All anyone ever had to do to escape punishment was to offer a pinch of incense into a brazier before a statue of the Emperor. One simply needed to accept society's norms of respect towards the divine Emperor. Simply that. Martyrdom was eminently voluntary. Now even those circumstances are a thing of the past and the new Emperor has ordered that Christians are not to be sought out for punishment at all. And I'm on the best of terms with many Christians. They welcome friends in high places and have even invited me to attend their religious functions."

This really was too much. Did the world really contain people who turned the other cheek? And were there people who would turn the other cheek to a man who had crucified friends and loved ones?

"You'll want to come with me to one of the Christians' ceremonies," continued Cato. You'd be most welcome. Since so many horrid rumors have spread among the populace, the Christians are very anxious for outsiders to see that they have nothing to hide. We'll attend a *missa*."

"Gladly. Whatever that is. But tell me something. You seem to think the Christians are perfectly harmless. Why, by the gods, are they persecuted so?"

"The gods have surprisingly little to do with the matter." Cato smiled as he munched some grapes. "I'll do you the great favor, while answering your question, of talking to you the way lawyers talk to one another in private. I'll first give you the official explanation, then the real explanation. Officially, Christians make themselves outcasts by shunning all participation in the state religion and thereby bringing down the anger of the gods on everyone. They're seen as haters of mankind for predicting an imminent end to the world, and as blasphemers for insisting that God came to earth in the form of a man to do the impossible. Now for the real reason.

"All over the Empire there are *collegia*, basically clubs where people who have a particular common interest band together for amusement, a sense of belonging, a sense of purpose, and the assurance of a decent burial. Bakers, blacksmiths, acrobats, charioteering fans, Christians, they all have their burial societies, in other words their *collegia*. But it's in the nature of government to be mistrustful of any organization that's not its own, not so? The imperial government is very mistrustful indeed, especially of organizations without the all-important stamp of antiquity. At one point the decision was even made not to permit new volunteer fire brigades!" Theophilus widened his eyes in surprise. "Yes, it's really so. The state distrusts all associations, all *collegia*, but if it has to accept any, it prefers those with an old tradition, a small following, and a narrow range of interests with no claim to universality. Christianity loses on all three counts! So, it sometimes transpires that the Christian of the Roman Empire burn. A volunteer fire brigade of a different sort, you might say!"

Theophilus ignored the tasteless jest. "It's sort of sad, really," he said. "Simple folk are so desperate for some hint of brightness in their lives that they'll listen to anyone who gives them tales of wonders and miracles."

"Are you so ready, then, to completely discount miracles?" asked Cato.

"I won't deny any phenomenon entirely, but miracles nearly so. I think the world will eventually outgrow belief in them."

"Then you must be an admirer of Epicurus."

"Of all the philosophers, he's my favorite."

Cato pushed forward a bowl of grapes. "Then eat, drink, and be merry, for tomorrow you may die!"

"Now, he never said that! There are scrolls and scrolls of Epicurus' writings, yet all that people tend to remember is that! I'll be glad to discuss him with you sometime; he's so misunderstood. And who is your favorite philosopher, Cato?"

"Plato! Is there really anyone else? I'm such a lover of Plato that I was overjoyed when I found one roundabout reference to Plato in the Christians' books. In the *Book of Mark*, Jesus comes to Jericho, which, I found out, symbolizes the lowly realm of the moon and the material world. There Jesus heals a blind beggar, a Platonic symbol of the blindness of the material world. The beggar is named Bartimaeus, *son of Timaeus*. Timaeus, as you know, is the name of Plato's most mystical book."

"Ah, there's so much of interest, to look forward to learning in the east!"

"I dare say, Now then, we were on the subject of miracles. I'd not be willing to wager that you'll find any evidence for miracles during your research, but I'd not discount miracles entirely either. Absurd stories abound, then suddenly there's one that sober men will swear they witnessed. Emperor Vespasian laughed off miracles, then one day a blind man and one with a withered hand begged him to use his spittle to heal them. He laughed in that hearty way of his and said, *Why not?* figuring that with his extraordinary luck it might actually work. And it did! He healed the blind and crippled with his spittle just as Jesus did! There you have it: just like Jesus the Emperor Vespasian performed a miracle, a *dynamis*, a *mighty act*!"

"So you're a believer in the supernatural?" asked Theophilus.

"I'll answer by quoting the original Cato, great Cato for whom people nicknamed me. He said he wondered how two soothsayers could pass each other in the street without breaking out into guffaws.

Theophilus laughed over the quip somewhat more than it deserved. The wine was having an effect. Then he suddenly thought to ask, "Say, why are you named after that grouchy old buzzard of the Republic, Cato, anyway? You're a Greek scholar and Cato hated Greek culture and refused to learn Greek till his old age."

"That's exactly why I was nicknamed Cato: because as a child I made such a fuss over my Greek lessons! But now, just like old Cato, at my advanced age I'm willing to look into any subject whatever."

"That's clear enough!" Theophilus pondered a moment. "Now, if that's the case, Cato, why don't you come with me to Judea to find the real Jesus?"

"Labors of Hercules! Do you think a man of my age is up to a trip like that?"

"Absolutely! Travel has never been easier! More people are doing it every year!"

"Then please pass me one olive."

"Why one olive?"

"Because the time I need to pit the olive is about how much time you'll need to talk me into making the trip!"

III RELISHING THE GODDESS

This day had been an excellent day of living life in the Roman way. Theophilus walked homeward well-fed and well-wined, and with his dizzied head pleasantly swimming in thoughts of upcoming travel, adventure and accomplishment. Only one more thing needed to be added in order to round out an excellent day in Rome. Theophilus wanted to fornicate.

To fornicate on this warm and pleasant eve would involve a visit to one of the very places that had given rise to the word: a fornix, the type of arched alcove frequented by prostitutes.

What could be more Roman? A prostitute of that class was known as a lupa, a "she-wolf." And a she-wolf was the very creature that suckled the little foundlings Romulus and Remus who founded Rome. A she-wolf was Rome's symbol.

Yes, it was all very Roman. Theophilus spotted a familiar long row of outdoor arches, the ultimate expression of Roman architecture and Roman desires. Each fornix housed a tempting meretrix, the Latin word for "earner" in its female form.

Theophilus paused to enjoy a scene of Rome at its bucolic best. All looked so picturesque in the gentle luminescence of sunset. Sets of Rome's signature tall cypress trees and shorter bulbous canopied stone-pine trees rustled in a pleasant breeze. And pleasure beckoned with a shapely hand and a melodious voice from each *fornix*.

Shopping and selecting were delicious joys, but this time Theophilus very quickly set eyes on one particular *lupa* and knew that this night he would have no other. She was young and beautiful, as practitioners of this extremely active and competitive trade often were, even in a moderately priced arcade like this one. She looked to be a German, and with the exchange of a few words her accent revealed that this was so. To Theophilus, she seemed perfect for now because of the way her long golden hair caught the sunlight in its waning minutes.

Theophilus gleefully undressed his *meretrix* and she purred hums that made an adequate similitude of enjoyment, too. They exchanged naked sexual caresses without a trace of self-consciousness out there in the wide-open fornix, as many other couples were doing all down the line. And far more than caresses were taking place; virtually no public act of eroticism, in this particular context, could engender shock in Rome.

Theophilus inspected the innumerable tiny blonde hairs on every part of the body of his young lady. In his pleasurable wine stupor these mundane objects were a source of fascination. They glinted so fetchingly in the special sunset light. Her skin was much better than wine. Theophilus enjoyed it with hands, lips and tongue. Her constant lovely singsong now bespoke either exceptional acting ability or genuine gratification. Theophilus now manually explored her pretty golden mons veneris and surmised that genuine gratification indeed it was, for she was a fount of wetness. She cried out and danced her hips enticingly as Theophilus explored her, little by little, ever deeper.

Theophilus mingled some gentle laughs with her sweet cries, because he knew that this was going to be an outstanding fornication. There followed much that was bliss for him, and, he hoped, for her. Interspersed with various acts were some words of negotiation and further exchanges of coinage. While she fellated him with vigor he surprised himself by calling out in much the same way she had. Then he wanted to mount her from the front to enjoy the feel of her moist depths while caressing her exquisite breasts, and from behind to enjoy the feel of even deeper moist depths while caressing her exquisite bottom. When he spurted deep within her, she sang out such a cry from an incomprehensible netherworld-otherworld that he knew he must experience the process all over again.

The second time he had her, again in all ways that he could imagine, he took time to notice even more detail on her wondrous body. And in this wise he noticed that she wore an amulet portraying a human body hanging on a tree. He asked her who was depicted and she answered with the name of a god whose name he knew just barely: Odin. She explained that Odin was wounded by a spear and hung on the World Tree to gain the secrets of the universe. As he penetrated her hard and long, from the previous angles as well as others, she seemed to be even more *in gush* with moisture than before, and even more eager to be deeply penetrated. She pulled on him rhythmically and hard to encourage his swelling penis to intrude much deeper inside her. Two bodies now covered in sweat thrashed about to feel, as completely as possible, each one the other. Theophilus found himself experiencing orgasms in series something like what he presumed a woman might have; he could only guess from her unceasing screams what his partner might be experiencing.

The ecstasy of his final spurt seemed to push him through a veil into a place where he had never been before. Suddenly he was awash in visions of arches of golden hue that were markers of endless bliss. And a torrent of words boomed through him, words that made no sense. Arch. Ark. Arcane. Archetype. Architecture. Archon. Arcana. And Greek arche: the origin of all things. He lay long in the arms of his meretrix, heaving breast on heaving breast, and wondered. But he knew that no answer would come, no not yet, and that it was unfair to take up more of her time without payment. So he bade this evening's fair young lady farewell and walked and wondered. What curtain had been drawn apart this day? The world seemed otherwise than it had been.

At Theophilus' lodgings, Titus his slave had stayed up late waiting for him, as expected. Theophilus saw him sitting in the dark, doing absolutely nothing but unwilling to wastefully light an oil lamp since in lamplight he would also be doing absolutely nothing anyway.

"A night of wine, is it?" Titus called out, semi-amiably. "So even a head-in-the-clouds student of philosophy will soak himself in wine from time to time! Bacchus be praised! I've often thought you should get drunk more often!"

Theophilus lit the wick on a small clay lamp filled with oil. His head hurt. He was a little resentful at Titus, who had probably drunk every bit as much wine as he, and of the worst imaginable quality, yet was his normal self, for whatever that was worth.

"Really, Master Theophilus, for all I knew you might have been lying dead in some alley!" Titus' voice seemed painfully loud. "It can easily happen when you go off carousing till all hours! And I asked the housekeeper over and over to keep your supper warm, making a real pest of myself, all for nothing!"

"You're making a pest of yourself right now, all for nothing! Why can't you behave like a slave, anyway?" Theophilus, dead tired, made ready to go to bed with his clothes on.

"What are you doing!?" Titus, though not a paragon of neatness himself, performed his not-excessive duties with pride, and was appalled at this lack of decorum, so he dashed to where he could start unlacing Theophilus' sandals. "Great Caesar, you'd be sleeping in your clothes like a shepherd if you didn't have somebody to look after you! Always it was the same, since you were in diapers, you wouldn't listen to anybody, you wouldn't tell anybody where you were going! A willful boy!" He threw the sandals under the bed.

"If you'll stop gabbing for a moment, I'll tell you where we're both going. Right back to Greece."

"What? Whatever for? We've barely been back in Italy for a year!"

"We'll be going through Greece on our way further east. I'm going to write a book about the east, and that's all you need to know for now."

Titus muttered some diffuse complaints out of habit and Theophilus spoke firmly over them. "You had no problem enjoying Greece like a true satyr, and I'm sure you'll be no less a satyr in the east. New wines to try out! New women to try out!"

"Ah, talk of wine and women from the young master," cackled Titus, "And you'd call me a satyr!"

Was there nothing this slave would not dare say? Hardly, since he was, when Theophilus thought about it, the only living human being who had known Theophilus in diapers. He was Theophilus' entire family, pondered Theophilus as he bade the old fellow to go to sleep.

This had been an exceptionally long day, an extraordinary day. Once prone on the webbing of his cot Theophilus fell asleep instantly and dreamed dreams unlike dreams he had ever dreamed before. They were not readily interpretable. For they were very oriental in nature and Theophilus had not yet been to the orient.

IV ABHORRING THE GORE

On the next occasion when a spectacle was scheduled, Theophilus accompanied fifty thousand other Romans to the Colosseum. On this beautiful sunny day, the amphitheater's open-air interior was richly colored by the sunlight streaming through the huge multicolored awning high above. On those heights sailors clambered about, arranging the gargantuan canvasses for the maximum benefit of spectators who wanted to enjoy their spectacle in the shade. Everything possible was being done to make the Romans happy. Exquisite fountains shot scented mists high in the air to cool them. Musicians labored avidly to soothe them, and acrobats and jugglers to amuse them. But what they had come for was blood.

The Roman crowd always kept its ruler at its mercy with an ever-present threat of violence that was a sort of parody of democracy. Rome's huge previouslyunheard-of seething concentration of a million humans could dethrone any emperor if sufficiently incensed. After free grain, free entertainment was the most effective means of keeping the huge rabble subdued. The rabble tended to become jaded, though, and ever more elaborate spectacles were required. As a matter of fact, Theophilus himself was amazed at how accustomed he had become to grandiose sights and sounds after only a few months in Rome.

In the arena several blindfolded horseback riders attempted to unsaddle one another with spears. No deaths occurred, only a few unpleasant injuries. The crowd mostly talked and fidgeted during this tame preliminary. Several giraffes came bounding out onto the sand. Theophilus gaped. He had never seen the like. The crowd seemed to like the beasts, but they were shot down by archers rather easily and the entertainment was all too brief. The beautiful creatures were dragged out with ropes tied to their feet.

Before long, human beings were dragged out in an identical manner. A few of the standard Thracians in their distinctive crested helmets fought the usual *retiarii* who carried nets and tridents. Blood liberally sprinkled the sand and Rome cheered every well-aimed slice and thrust. Then came a special feature: a great favorite among the gladiators battled a tiger, an exceedingly rare attraction. The celebrated professional killer made too short work of his adversary, however. The mob hooted disapproval. Yesterday's star would be tomorrow's has-been, a fighter who would now be likely to receive the dreaded thumbs-outward gesture, *pollex verso,* when next he appealed to the audience for his life. Then came more Thracians and *retiarii*, each eager to attain stardom, each likely to be dragged out dead by the heels before many months had passed.

Theophilus wondered why he was sitting here. Initial fascination with gladiatorial games was giving way to disgust. Noble animals being slaughtered for a momentary thrill was bad enough, but amusement derived from green guts spilling out of human beings was unspeakable. He was satiated, no longer able to justify the games in his own mind with the old excuse that some few of the participants obtained great fame and fortune.

But he was here and had been here many times before, juggling that same poor justification, a man no better than the rest. He came for the thrill, as did all these other human beasts. No, he thought, humans were worse than beasts. Beasts were insentient and hence blameless. Humans, on the other hand, inflicted cruelty on both man and beast while displaying the effrontery to pretend the proceedings had a religious significance.

Worse than beasts. Theophilus, wistful, distracted, went over in his mind how this Colosseum had come to be. He mused how he might give schoolchildren a quick history of the Roman Empire, using a lineup of imperial busts that was in view.

Emperor Augustus, with his somewhat odd triangular head, of which sculptors strove to make handsome versions to distribute all over the Empire. He brought to a war-weary, world peace: the *Pax Romana*. The Empire thrived.

Emperor Tiberius, a fine young-looking head, not the head of a debauched old man who shut himself up on the Isle of Capri and was despised by all. Tiberius' bloodthirsty deputy Sejanus took overrule of the Empire, and put an end to the promise of heaven on earth that had been so vociferously proclaimed by Augustus' propaganda.

Emperor Caligula, another fine young triangle-head, one that did not hint at the evil therein. Augustus and Tiberius had called themselves princeps, the first among equals, dedicated to the service of all. When Caligula became princeps the sham showed itself all too clearly for what it was "I can do anything to anyone," said Caligula, demonstrating that he meant what he said for as long as people remained too cowed to assassinate him. But in the end, of course, assassinate him they did.

Emperor Claudius, looking neither foolish nor wise, the two things that he was reputed to be. He made humanity look governable again. His big mistake was letting himself be talked into appointing as his heir Nero, who forthwith had him assassinated.

Emperor Nero, surnamed Ahenobarbus meaning "red beard," whose bushy hair and bushy sideburns made him stand out among the busts, as did the hint of a sneer. Megalomaniac though he was, this emperor's first five years as emperor were harmonious and calm. But Nero's subsequent years were a nightmare. Eventually this madman plunged the Roman world into a civil war from which it barely emerged intact.

Emperor Vespasian, who looked like everyone's most personable and most sagacious uncle. This was the general who picked up the pieces after the civil war. A breath of fresh air after his predecessors, he reversed their technique: He did not take himself seriously, but instead took his duties seriously. As Emperor, he brought order and hope.

Emperor Titus, who resembled his father Vespasian, only in burlier form. Although his reign was short, he finished his father's main building project, the Colosseum. This structure was actually called the Flavian Amphitheater, named after the imperial family, but it was popularly known as the Colosseum because of the colossal statue next to it. This was a statue of Nero that had been transformed into a statue of Apollo. Nero had been widely known as the Beast. Could the Beast be transformed into a being of light? Could the human lust for blood be confined artificially to the Colosseum? As it turned out, no.

Emperor Domitian, whose look of fear mixed with cunning had been captured by the artist. This was Vespasian's woebegone evil son, the ruler who enjoyed sitting in his room for hours spearing flies with a stylus, and who soon turned to slaughtering innocent thousands. The loathsome imperial story had made its cyclical turn once more. Domitian had been assassinated not many years before.

Theophilus inspected the handsome amphitheater so caked with blood. It was as though humanity had constructed the place to mock its own situation: a circular depravity show punctuated by screams of agony and cheers. He wondered if in a thousand years man would be no better, still trapped, still monstrous, still unworthy of calling himself civilized.

Theophilus looked at the Colosseum's ornate empty seat reserved for the emperor. Emperor Nerva, really too old to be appointed Emperor in the first place, had recently died. Now a military man named Marcus Ulpius Traianus, commonly known as Trajan, was being hailed as the new emperor and new savior. He was still far away. His entry into Rome was eagerly awaited: another savior. Another savior? Theophilus felt such an act had been listed on the Colosseum's program too many times already.

Where was the desperately needed savior? So much of the Jesus "good news" story seemed nonsense, but much else seemed precious, unforgettable, and even indispensable. Visions of the Good Samaritan haunted Theophilus till he walked out of the amphitheater for the last time ever. If ever he craved exciting spectacle there was another place where he could go. He would satisfy his craving for exciting shows with chariot races from now on.

However, a last thought concerning the Colosseum haunted him. He wanted to find something. He searched the outside of the Colosseum for an inscription that he vaguely remembered having seen. He found the inscription and inspected it and confirmed that it said what he had thought it said.

IMPERATOR TITVS CAESAR VESPASIANVS
AVGVSTVS AMPHITHEATRVM NOVVM EX MANVBIS
FIERI IVSSIT
"Emperor Titus Caesar Vespasian Augustus constructed this new amphitheater with the spoils of war."

The inscription made plain that Emperor Titus Caesar had funded the construction of the Colosseum with the spoils looted from the Jerusalem Temple. This seemed to matter deeply, but he had no idea why.

V INSPECTING THE TREASURE

Theophilus felt that a cleansing was in order after his attendance at the Colosseum. At first he made for the baths, but changed his mind and went to look for an address that Cato had given him.

When he knocked with his foot on what he hoped was the right door, a man answered who was so small that he seemed to be mostly white beard and frown.

"Are you the Syrian rabbi?" asked Theophilus.

The frown deepened. "Yes. And you must be the friend of Cato I've been told to expect: Lover-of-God?"

"Theophilus."

The little man grunted. Even the grunt was in an awfully exotic accent to Theophilus' ears. The man motioned for Theophilus to come inside, though seemingly with the greatest of reluctance.

Inside the humble abode, the Syrian rabbi suddenly turned to address his guest as though he were an errant schoolboy. "Son, do you know what a 'week' is?"

Theophilus stifled his chagrin at being subjected to a test on oriental folklore and replied, "Certainly. A week arranges days into groups of seven, so that each day represents one of the heavenly bodies: Saturn's day, the sun's day, the moon's day, Mars' day,

Mercury's day, Venus' day, Jupiter's day."

The rabbi looked no less displeased. "Hmm. I wouldn't have put it quite that way. Come with me."

The rabbi led Theophilus into his other room. The first little room had all the jam-packed accoutrements of a room that was lived in. The other little room was packed from floor to ceiling with books. The rabbi carefully took down one volume. He showed Theophilus the first words on this scroll.

"You want to study the holy books, and I'm pointing out the words that the holy books start with. Those words will help you get something important straight right away. 'In the beginning, God created heaven and earth.' Then, look, it goes on to say that God created creation in six days and on the seventh day he rested. That is why we have weeks, young man. To commemorate God's creation we do not work on the seventh day which we call the Sabbath, which is what you call Saturn's day, which is today, so you shouldn't have come, and I hope that you'll kindly refrain from doing so again!"

Theophilus' lips tightened. It was all well and good to honor God on Saturn's day for accomplishing the creation, but how was he supposed to know about the custom? In his mind's eye he saw the gold that he had intended to donate to this man's synagogue metamorphosing into silver.

But the lessons were about to begin, despite the Sabbath, so announced the rabbi in firm schoolmaster's tones. Though harsh of voice, he now very gently handled his books.

"In Greek we call our Jewish holy books simply biblia, 'the books.' There are twenty-two of them, the same number as the number of letters in the Hebrew alphabet. The Greek translation of the biblia that you'll be reading is called the Septuagint, or simply the LXX, because it was supposedly translated by 70 scholars in 70 days." Others say 72 scholars in 72 days. Either way, those numbers are astrological numbers having to do with something called decans. He added with something of a smirk, "The

Septuagint mentions people who are titled 'Christ,' meaning 'the anointed one,' about 40 times, so somehow I doubt that your Christians are really onto anything new."

"I believe the Christians also refer to their holy books as the biblia, do they not?"

"I'll thank you not to compare those books to these books in my presence, whatever you may care to do elsewhere!" groused the rabbi. "But sometime I'll show you something which should help open your eyes. I'll show you our scribes at work. When they copy the holy books, the most careful and scrupulous ceremony is required, including the enunciation of every word as it is copied, and the destruction of any work that is to the slightest degree tainted by error. If you insist on studying the Christians' absurd scribblings, on the other hand, you'll find that hardly any two texts agree! One Christian adds whatever comes into his head, another subtracts what he doesn't like, and a third splatters commentary all over the margins which is later incorporated as original material into the text by a fourth!"

"I'll beware."

The rabbi grunted and continued his lecture. "We categorize our holy books into three parts. These scrolls you see here are the Wisdom Literature. Over here are the books called the Prophets, which are held in somewhat higher regard. Most holy of all are the first five books of the collection of twenty-two. We call these first five books the Torah, the Law. Those books which are not Torah you can come here and read whenever you please."

"Except on 'Saturn's day.'"

"Correct. But the Torah itself will have to be read to you by one of my assistants. I'm afraid I can't permit it to be touched by a gentile."

"Ah, yes, a non-Jew. As a gentile am I still to address you as 'rabbi'?"

"Well, I'll admit it sounds a bit strange coming from you. It's Hebrew for 'my teacher.' But yes, that's how you should address me. Nothing else is apt. I've been a teacher almost all my life."

That much at least was obvious.

Theophilus inquired, "May I ask, rabbi, if you are also to be considered a priest of your religion?"

Sadness showed in the deep brown eyes. "We Jews have had no priesthood since the fall of the Temple. This is our priesthood and our temple!" He indicated his room full of books. "The books! The law! Those who are learned in the books may be addressed as rabbi, but the books themselves are the priesthood and the temple." He caressed his books. "We are a wandering people, with no place to call home. Three times we've been expelled from Rome alone. Only these books are our home. And you are welcome to visit our home."

The Syrian rabbi had begun to sound profoundly more congenial. To Theophilus appeared the image of his silver turning back into gold.

Gold.

It was peculiar. Theophilus did not think of himself as a money-hungry person. Why then, did his thoughts lately keep turning to gold? No. He had a feeling that it was not a matter of gold in the monetary sense at all. All at once a bolt of intuition struck him. The rabbi's talk of the Jews' lost Jerusalem and the Jews' lost Temple had reminded him that there was something that he needed to see. And that something was golden. He needed to see Rome's most sumptuous display of gold. He took leave of the Syrian rabbi with regards that were commensurate with golden feelings. Then he headed for Vespasian's Temple of Peace.

Emperor Vespasian had come to power during the post-Nero upheavals that led to the Jews' expulsion from Judea. He had rushed to Rome to be proclaimed Emperor and had assigned to his son Titus the reckoning with rebellious Judea. This task involved the destruction of the Temple of Jerusalem, which was reputed to be the most impressive religious edifice in all the world. Titus brought the looted treasures of the Temple of Jerusalem, and they were now kept in Vespasian's Temple of Peace. Rome liked to make permanent boast that it had brought peace to the world, so there was Augustus's Altar of Peace and Vespasian's Temple of Peace. Since Rome also liked to make permanent boast of its conquests, the treasures of the Temple of Jerusalem were on display to the public.

Peace was Emperor Vespasian's legacy. He had brought peace back to the Roman Empire after one of Rome's most difficult times. Numerous coins still existed that told the tale with utmost simplicity: on one side was a profile portrait of Emperor Vespasian, and on the other side the word PAX. The Temple of Peace was meant to make the statement that Emperor Vespasian had united all the world in peace. But this was done in the Roman way: the temple displayed all the world's booty! And loot from the obliterated Temple in Jerusalem was the central exhibit.

Theophilus entered the great square edifice and walked through a courtyard defined by pillars of pink Egyptian marble. The courtyard was full of fountains and particularly lush flower-bearing plants; it was a paradise garden that said "peace." It smelled peaceful. Here the Roman state had splurged on all kinds of scented flowers from all over the known world, flowers which blossomed and exuded aromas at all different times of year. The visitors, too, were colorful and came from all over the world: Celts in breeches, Asians in robes of many hues, Egyptians who shivered in their customary too-skimpy clothing. All had been united by Rome.

Theophilus headed for the room that displayed the Jerusalem Temple treasure. In this room he beheld golden treasures whose central piece was the famous candelabrum called the menorah. Situated on its spectacular bejeweled table, it reached beyond the height of most men, including Theophilus who was of average height. Such height was appropriate, since the object was said to symbolize the "lights" that were the seven main heavenly bodies. The other main exhibit in this "Jerusalem Temple Room" was the long solid-gold table for offerings called "showbread." All around were other spectacular objects of precious metal and jewels. This treasure overwhelmed. Theophilus had read in the works of several authors who had seen the world that there was nothing in the world like these objects. He recalled that there was a common belief that Jerusalem was the holiest place on earth. So should Jerusalem not have had the most exquisite treasure?

Standing and staring, Theophilus felt that this holy panoply of wonders exerted on him some sort of otherworldly pull. The feeling had everything to do with his recent inexplicable mental encounters with the notion of gold being something much more than gold. He was startled when the realization came to him that not even Jesus in his time would have been allowed to look at this treasure! And now he, humble obscure Theophilus, could drink it in as much of the sight as he pleased!

There were many mysterious aspects to the allure of this treasure. So Theophilus stood there for a very long time and mused. Ultimately strange voices spoke to him Arch. Ark. Arcane. Archetype. Architecture. Archon. Arcana. *Arche*. The words echoed. Something was missing here. He tried and tried, feeling sure that he was on the verge of a revelation. All at once a spark of incite did deign to come to him. Yes. Something was beginning to make sense! The most important part of the treasure, the most important part by far, was missing! It was the Ark of the Covenant!

VI MEETING THE BEAST

And before long, a sort of golden gate was opened for him once again. At Cato's invitation, Theophilus attended exclusive festival celebrations at a stunning portion of the remains of Nero's notorious extravagance: the Golden House. Amidst all the guests' finery Theophilus' excellent eyes immediately zeroed in on one distant sartorial object of gold. It was a depiction of the candelabrum of the Jerusalem Temple, and it hung from the neck of an older woman who was notably attractive despite her years, and whose demeanor announced that she was well aware of that central feature of her life, her attractiveness.

Cato noticed the direction in which Theophilus was staring, and suggested, "You really must talk to her, that, I would say, alluring-despite-her-age matron there. Her name is Floralia. She has her ways of knowing everything that goes on in Rome. And she is an ardent *judaizer*."

"She must be very well-connected indeed, to be a Jewish woman at such an exclusive gathering."

"No, she's not Jewish. She has as thoroughly Roman a pedigree as anyone in Rome. A 'judaizer' is a Roman who admires and practices elements of the Jewish forms of worship."

Theophilus approached Floralia and was gratified that her

"come hither" look became gradually more unmistakable. She had impeccable style and her expensive perfume was intoxicating. Theophilus let a decent interval of small talk pass before he expressed admiration for her silk gown which was dyed a rare bright shade of green, and stroked it ever so gently in order to be suggestive. Her smiling reaction brightened his hopes as to where this conversation might lead. But for now he led the conversation elsewhere: first to the topic of how impossibly distant was the Land of Silk, so that no one had any reliable information about the place, then to the topic of his own upcoming adventure in Judea, which was no longer considered terribly exotic as travel was becoming easier and easier. He then asked Floralia what it meant to be a judaizer.

The nose was strong and aquiline. The forceful eyes were a daughter-of-the-earth light brown. The hair was done up in a labor-intensive tower and was colored with red henna as was de rigeur in this time and place. All bespoke a lifetime of enormous care taken in appearances. Floralia was from head to toe a wealthy Roman. But her reply shattered all that her image averred.

"Many who have seen Rome's state religion steadily lose all of its credibility and all of its zest have come to take comfort in the very ancient practices of the Jews. And the Christian writings are Jewish writings as far as we curious Romans are concerned. I myself first became interested in such writings when I heard about one particular passage. The passage is Matthew having Jesus preach very simply and sweetly to the Jews. *You should love the Lord God with your whole heart, your whole soul, and your whole mind. This is the greatest and the first commandment. And the second is much like it. Love your neighbor as yourself. The whole of the law and the prophets derive from these two.*"

Theophilus was quick with a compliment. "You seem to have some familiarity with these things. So tell me. Was Jesus the greatest prophet of the Jews? Was he their savior? Why do some of them worship him and others hate him?"

Floralia waved her hand dismissively and made the fine robe swish. "Oh, I really don't care about all those debates. They're endless and boring. I simply read whatever appeals to me and use whatever elements of ceremony and worship and devotion that call out to me. Let others debate. You can find absolutely any interpretation of Jesus that you want. Some claim that Jesus was God or nearly God. Others claim that he didn't exist at all."

"I find both theories rather far-fetched. The claim that Jesus didn't exist at all sounds suspiciously like a too-easy way to discredit all Christian writings all at once."

"Well, who knows? All of that sort of doctrinal squabbling leads nowhere and doesn't interest me at all. If you're going east to look for the real Jesus I think that you may find yourself living a famous anecdote. The anecdote concerns a researcher who sought to discover whether Homer really wrote the Iliad. The researcher ended up finding out that the Iliad was written by a different author with the same name!"

She was quite a delight to talk to, thought Theophilus with a smile. He said, "Our mutual acquaintance Cato seems to think that Jesus was mostly an embellishment. Under his theory the embellishment of Jesus the prophet was carried out by Jews to counter Virgil's propaganda campaign to posit Augustus as a savior, a god, a Prince of Peace and so on."

"Augustus seems to be only the first of many possible prototypes of Jesus. How about Hercules as such a prototype? Hercules was born of a virgin and his father was a god, a 'god the father' to whom Hercules ascended after his death. Hercules was called the Good Shepherd, a savior, a Prince of Peace. Often, he is depicted in art as a baby being held by Hera, the Earth Mother. The name Hercules means 'Mother Nature's Glory.' Hercules is earth's activity and fulfillment. He defeats such villainous foes as earth-boundness, multiplicity, death, confusion and so on. A god, a man or a legend? Who knows? Plenty of historians regard Hercules as a historical figure who went around performing fabulous feats.

Herodotus thought so. Look, Theophilus, the great Herodotus himself unhesitatingly reported that the god Attis was a real king who died while hunting, and that the god Horus was a real king who ruled Egypt. Pointless debate and conjecture without end! But you want to know about such things and hear about such things. So I know just what to do. Come home with me and I'll show you something of interest!"

He could hardly have hoped for more. Soon he was joining Floralia for excellent wine on plush red pillows in her boudoir. She directed a slave where to find a certain tablet bearing a list, and soon she was showing it and explaining it to Theophilus.

"This list originally came to me long ago from Cato. How that man loves to make lists! The list is labeled as *Aretology*."

"Aretology. A wonder-laden biography in which the hero is half-man and half-god and is a Son of God whose miraculous birth is announced by angels, and who comes to save the world."

"Yes, quite so. It's a type of myth that applied to Moses, Alexander, Pythagoras, Empedocles, Apollonius of Tyana and many others. Here is a list of the basic features of that widespread myth."

The list read:

> I: Mother is a royal virgin.
> II: Father is a king.
> III: Unusual conception.
> IV: Reputed to be a son of a god.
> V: There are attempts to kill him.
> VI: Raised by foster parents in a primitive faraway
>   country.
> VII: No details of childhood.
> VIII: Becomes a king.
> IX: Decrees laws.
> X: There transpires a loss of favor on the part of his
>   subjects.

XI: Driven from his throne and from his city.
XII: A mysterious death at the top of a hill.
XIII: Not succeeded by his children.
XIV: His body is not buried.
XV: Nonetheless he has one or more holy sepulchers.

Theophilus' reaction to the list was, "Hercules! This is quite an impressive list. It makes me wonder if I'm really just wasting my time by going east to find out the truth about Jesus. It seems that Jesus may have been just another holy man whose life story was puffed up to make him seem a great spiritual hero like so many other great spiritual heroes!"

"Not quite like the others," countered Floralia. "The difference is that Jesus was the one among those spiritual heroes who belonged to the Jews! The Jews are special. Why do you think there exists such a thing as judaizers among us Romans?"

"I certainly would like to know why." Theophilus crossed his arms made himself comfortable on Floralia's mountain of pillows to hear what she had to say.

"Historically the Jews started out as very few but very special. Josephus, the chronicler of the Jews for the Romans, related the Jews' origins in his writings. The original *'Ioudaioi' id est* the first Jews, were those Hebrews who returned from Babylonian exile, with Persian backing, to re-establish worship at the Temple of Jerusalem. For heaven's sake don't pay any attention to Tacitus' silly story that the Jews are called Jews because they first came from Mount Ida in Crete! Those Hebrews who came back from Babylonian exile and remained rural and did not come up to the exacting standards of the *Ioudaioi* became Samaritans; and Mount Gerizim became the Samaritans' shrine. But who, on Jupiter's earth, ever cared about Mount Gerizim? One can find holy spots everywhere, but many believe that Jerusalem is the holiest ground on earth. The Jews became who they were because they were the custodians of Jerusalem. They were heirs to all of the mystical traditions of the nation known as Israel, but most of that nation disappeared, and all that remained were the Samaritans and the Jews. And the Jews were the Israelites who were the keepers of Jerusalem. At a time when the world was rapidly becoming more united and more cosmopolitan, the Jews were special because they were the heirs to the power of Israel and the power of the world's holiest ground."

"I know where this is going, Floralia." He wondered if she noticed how he kept eying her up and down, in hopes that there were somewhere else where the conversation was going. "Along came us Romans, whom the Jews considered loutish and barely civilized, but there was no denying that we were powerful. We Romans were impressed by the culture of the Greeks. But from all that I've read the Jews instilled in us an even deeper awe: the awe and dread of a people with the very deepest spiritual power."

The judaizer nodded. "Correct. There was a deepseated superstitious need to harness that power. But I shouldn't call it mere superstition. There is something that anyone who studies these matters eventually finds out: that there is a deep mystical connection between the power of Rome and the power of Jerusalem. Insiders were always aware of how much Julius Caesar and Augustus depended on the secret machinations of loyal Jews to establish the Roman Empire. And to keep it running! And scholarly Emperor Claudius had as his best friend and closest confidant a Jew, namely Herod Agrippa.

"Claudius was extreme in his friendship with Jews, but such friendship was a custom that other Roman rulers had started. That's the same Claudius who ordered all Druids exterminated and even ordered the execution of a man whom he saw wearing a Druid's talisman! Never was there anything but antipathy between Roman and Celt. But between Roman and Jew there always existed a complicated interdependence. Josephus was the main literary enabler of this RomanJewish alliance, but Luke was another. Look closely and you'll see a lot of material from

Josephus' writings in Luke. Certain names ring out: Quirinius, Herod Agrippa, Felix, the tetrarch Lysanius, and three particular Jewish rebel leaders. Luke is widely seen as being anti-Jewish in what he wrote, but that's only true to the uninitiated. The fact was, Luke endeavored to demonize certain cabals of Jews and promote other cabals of Jews.

"Claudius made his Jewish best friend, Herod Agrippa the ruler of Judea. And note that combined Jewish-Roman name: Herod Agrippa. Herod Agrippa met a curious end that is described in the *Book of Acts*. First he beheaded the apostle named James. And seeing that that pleased the rabble he imprisoned Peter. But Peter made a miraculous escape from prison, with an angel removing his shackles. Then Herod Agrippa, the crowd's darling, appeared before the crowd dressed in dazzling silver at a festival in honor of Claudius, and they hailed him as a living god. In retribution, God struck Herod Agrippa dead, dead by being eaten alive by worms, of all things!"

Theophilus shook his head. "Is there any truth to any of that?"

"Well, who can ever know for sure? What can one say? The point was that some tale-maker or other felt the need to show that Peter and not Herod Agrippa was the true heir to the mysterious Rome-Jerusalem power nexus!"

"Did you ever meet Peter or Paul?" asked Theophilus.

"No, but I did know three people who figure in Christian scriptures and thus will likely be famous names throughout the centuries. And that's rather amusing, isn't it? This tale is a little complex, but listen closely and you'll get it, and you'll be a long way towards figuring out the things that you want to figure out.

"The first person I knew who figured in the Christian scriptures was Lydia of Thyatira. She was a wealthy convert to Christianity and was a person rather a lot like me. You can find her in the *Book of Acts*. Lydia owned a business that manufactured purple cloth. She was a paragon of fashion and not at all the sort of person who you would suppose would be attracted to Paul the street barker. Her wealth did a great deal to further the cause of Paul. She was important enough to be mentioned in a second Christian book, the *Book of Revelation*. Because whoever wrote the *Book of Revelation* obviously hated a great many things, and among the many things he hated was Paul. That's precisely the opposite of Luke, who propagandized for Paul! The author of the *Book of Revelation* condemned both Paul and Lydia under code names. Somewhere amidst his apocalyptic ranting, where he was supposedly addressing the lapsed Christians of Thyatira, the author of the *Book of Revelation* attacked both Paul and Lydia. He cursed Paul while using the name *Balaam*, because Balaam was an ancient pseudo-prophet who was in no way true to the faith of Israel, and he cursed Lydia by using the name 'Jezebel,' because Jezebel was the customary name with which to curse a non-Jewish harlot.

Theophilus rubbed his chin. "Fascinating. A couple of examples of supposed holy writ that is really nothing more than petty grudge-based name-calling! I'll keep your tale about Lydia in mind. And who was the other acquaintance of yours who made it into Christian Holy Scripture?"

Floralia wore a bemused expression. "The other person was Josephus himself! And the author who placed one of my friends, this time Josephus, in Christian Holy Scripture was once again that dyspeptic loony who wrote the *Book of Revelation*. The loony condemned Lydia, under the name of Jezebel, for prophesying and for preaching immorality such as consuming food that had been sacrificed to idols. He condemned Josephus rather more vehemently. He condemned Josephus as the *False Prophet* who espoused surrender to 'the Beast,' which is to say surrender to *Rome*! The *Book of Revelation* thundered on about how the Beast would decree that no one could buy or sell without the *Mark of the Beast* on the right hand and forehead. This was an actual prayer device called a phylactery that was sanctioned by the Rome-backed Temple priesthood: a box containing prayers that connected, by means of a strap, the right hand and the forehead. In Matthew, Jesus expressed disapproval of this new vogue for phylacteries."

"A convoluted mess, like all politics. Some Jews are in league with Rome, and others referred to Rome as 'the Beast,' the very worst term in all of their scriptures."

Floralia's light laugh was a delight. "Well, I did say that it was an extremely complex family relationship! But keep one idea in mind to make things clearer. You see, the *Book of Revelation* is the text for those Jews who hated any hint of compromise with Rome and hated the pro-Rome compromisers such as Josephus and Paul. I think it is worth knowing what that book is all about, because, inane as it is, it's gaining more attention all the time, with interpretation that are sometimes even zanier than the original text. I know it's confusing, but I think I've made the point that that incredible nightmare-like *Book of Revelation* can make more sense if you see it as an elaborate code for condemning Rome, Josephus, Paul, and the whole pro-Roman Rome-Jewish nexus."

"Floralia, you really should set down on papyrus these interesting tidbits that you know. It's all so valuable for historians!"

She waved her hand dismissively. "You know how I feel about such things. But I will tell you the fascinating story of Josephus, and you can be the one to write it down if you wish. Josephus is a topic you certainly should know about. Too bad you missed meeting him. It wasn't so long ago that he died. Quite a man. Quite a man. He had the ancestry and looks and voice and abilities and attitudes of a prophet. Just as much as Paul he was a crucial link in the all-powerful Rome-Jerusalem nexus."

"More so than Peter?"

"Just listen. Forget that damned Peter. There have always been prophecies that men who will come out of Judea will rule the world. So listen to what happened. Josephus was an extremely powerful man. He was in charge of the Jewish military forces of the Galilee during the Jewish rebellion in Nero's time. But he was a cunning Jacob, not a bullish Achilles. People were slaughtered in droves. Defeat was imminent. The leaders of the Galilee rebellion gathered in a hideout to decide what to do next. You may or may not know the incredible events that happened next."

"I do indeed know them, but I'd' love to hear them again from you."

"As golden tongued as Jacob, Josephus tricked all the other leaders into committing suicide while he himself lived on. Then he surrendered to General Vespasian. Can you imagine the amount of gall and heaven-sent good fortune that Josephus had, in order to do what he did next? He convinced Vespasian that he, Josephus, was God's prophet, and that he, Vespasian, was hereby being prophesied by Josephus and selected by God to rule the world! Josephus harangued Vespasian into believing that God had destined him to be Emperor! And Josephus pulled it off! He combined the old belief that men will come out of Judea to rule the world, and an old prophecy about a star and a scepter from the east. And he pulled it off!"

"Yes, it's a classic story. A memorable and incredible story, which I'm always glad to hear from a slightly different point of view. And both Vespasian and his son Titus did become emperors, fulfilling the prophecy that men would come out of Judea to rule the world."

Floralia asserted, "That's just one superficial aspect of the fulfillment of the prophecy. Another is the proud Arch of Titus in the Forum with its depiction of the Temple's candelabrum being carried in triumph to Rome. Another is the stunning spectacle of the golden treasure of the Jerusalem Temple in Rome's Temple of Vespasian. You've seen that, no doubt?"

"Yes, I have. Marvelous."

"Beneath the surface, so much more was happening. A whole Jewish coterie stood behind Rome's rulers. Vespasian's most trusted military deputy was a nephew of the renowned Jewish philosopher Philo."

"Speaking of Philo, I'm reminded to ask about something that I consider highly important. Tell me what you think of this. There is no mention of Jesus in the three writers where one would be most likely to find such a mention: Philo, Josephus and Justus of Tiberias. Why?"

"Well, I'll tell you what I think of those three. Philo had a very aristocratic above-it-all attitude. So did Josephus once he was safely and comfortably ensconced in Vespasian's palace with admirers and a pension. In the days of Philo and Josephus, Jesus was considered a prophet for plebeians. That state of affairs did not change until recently, when Luke's books set out expressly to change it. As for Justus of Tiberias, well, I really don't know. The only thing I know about him is that he and Josephus couldn't stand one another; quite a natural state of affairs for two authors who were writing about the same time and place! Look, you can't expect serious historians to take seriously the fairy tales of the hoi polloi. The gospels mention that Jesus' death was followed by an earthquake, the darkening of the sun and moon, and the dead rising from the grave. Don't you think that historians would have reported such things if they had really happened?"

Theophilus said, "I'm sorry I missed meeting this man Josephus. But your chambers are a good place for me to try to picture him. A charismatic warrior-prophet-firebrand who deteriorated into an arrogant spoiled sybarite lolling around the palace on pillows and having slave girls feed him grapes."

"That picture is not too far off the mark. Yet he remained a charismatic and fascinating figure. In a way he was the ultimate traitor, but also in a way he was the savior of his people. He spent many years writing a history of the Jewish people in just such a careful and perfect way that pleased both the Roman ruling class and the Jewish ruling class and enabled those two groups to continue a cooperation that managed the great Empire beneath the surface. The emperors always stayed close to the washed-up

Herodian Jewish kings and their heirs, as close as possible without actually intermarrying with them. Emperor Titus was deeply in love with the Jewish princess Bernice. He wanted to marry her, but popular opinion drew the line. Such a marriage would have been as impossible as a marriage of Caesar to Cleopatra. But the Herodians hung on, carried around through the streets of Rome on their litters for decade after decade; so you could always see them and so you can still see them today."

Theophilus insisted, "They're of no interest to me at all, those has-beens. But tell me. The *Book of Acts* is so full of personages who lived not so long ago. Surely some among them were people that you knew, in addition to the ones you already mentioned."

"No, no others. But if you're tempted to go running around looking for the people mentioned in the Book of Acts, if I were you, I wouldn't take anything in the *Book of Acts* very seriously. It's not history but a novel. Everybody was writing novels back in Nero's glittery time. Nero made fictional literature thrive as never before, with all kinds of handouts and favors to novelists and poets and playwrights. The *Book of Acts* was a novel that set out to make some very definite points. We Romans have our novel, the *Satyricon*, in which Romans run around acting outrageous. And the Jews have their novel, the *Book of Acts*, in which Jews run around acting sanctimonious!

"By the way I wouldn't be so quick to dismiss the Herodians who seem to be so washed up. They still exercise a lot of power behind the scenes. *Satyricon* Jews! Believe me, Paul, the man you're so interested in, was nothing like the picture that Lucius Livinius Piso will present to you. Yes, I know all about your upcoming interview with Piso! Word gets around. Paul's so-called imprisonment in Rome was a joke. He was not a prisoner. No. He was being used. He was kept around like a useful trained circus hound. Paul was in as tight as could be with the Herodians. Look for evidence in the texts if you don't believe me. Look for a text where Paul claims as a friend someone named Herodion. A powerful clue, that, the fact that Paul would have a friend from the pro-Roman Herodian dynasty.

"And look at the end of Paul's *Letter to the Philippians* where he claims to have friends even in the imperial household. What a powerful clue is that! You can see all over Paul's career various traces of his being helped by friends in high places, traces like Drusilla the Jewish wife of the procurator Felix who sent Paul to Rome for a hearing instead of inflicting on him a punishment. Paul was a useful, cunning, barking, trained hound, that's what Paul was. I maintain that you'll find out that Paul was used by the Roman and Jewish powers-that-be to transform the martyred Jesus from a Jewish revolutionary into a *useful phantom*!"

Floralia stretched out languorously on some of her many pillows and let out the sigh of a luxury lover who had just become sated with one form of entertainment and desired another. It was as though she had spent too much time on one aspect of her being, the mental, and had suddenly remembered her liking for another aspect of her being, the physical. The two exchanged glances that mutually assured that they were getting ready to exchange one popular form of Roman amusement for another.

She asked Theophilus, "You're fond of the *Satyricon*, aren't you?" But she did not wait for an answer. She thrust her naked perfumed leg out suggestively from her green silk robe and place her hand strategically on her guest's robe to coax up the answer she was after.

Four hands now moved frenetically among the robes and pillows. Each new stage of near nakedness was another adventure to enjoy. As soon as the robes were clumps of discards on the floor and the two *Satyricon* Romans were a sculpted mound of nudity in bed, Floralia eagerly sought out Theophilus' penis to fellate him.

With a smile, she intoned, "Mouths can do so much more than endlessly jabber theology!" Then her words were muffled in a mouth that took in Theophilus rhythmically and fully.

She proved to be a woman with a fondness for semen, taking

Theophilus' hot liquid when it spurted into her mouth and
smearing it with gusto on various parts of her body. The glistening
liquid appeared to be an aphrodisiac for her. Caressing herself with
it made her shudder and moan, and she wanted to do everything
with her hands all at once. They found each other's rhythm. She
settled on rapidly stroking the carefully shaved area between her
legs.

Theophilus applied his tongue to that region and set her
thrashing. He had a difficult time hearing what she was yelling, but
finally ascertained that the word was "Kteis! Kteis!" In Greek she
was directing him to her clitoris. So he applied his tongue there,
and he had sensed her desire correctly so she thrashed and
screamed all the more.

When Theophilus began thrusting inside Floralia they had
positioned themselves partly upright on some of the many pillows.
Thus, with a good view of the room he noticed for the first time
that the room had a sculpted motif of many conch shells. He
pondered that this was obviously a motif that Floralia adored as
much as penises, and there was a good reason why. For the conch
was a symbol of Venus and a symbolic representation of the part of
the female anatomy to which it had an affinity both in appearance
and sound: the cunnus. Theophilus had stamina and treated Floralia
to a long spell of pleasuring during which she had ample
opportunity to emit various descriptions of the unearthly multiple
pleasures in her concha.

The night of many pillows proceeded with many caresses
which repeatedly transitioned into various suckings and
penetrations. At length, the last of the oil lamps flickered out.
Dawn filtered into the room through slatted blinds. By that soft
light Floralia played with Theophilus' member, playfully coaxing
out one last hint of an erection.

Kissing the phallus repeatedly, she made Theophilus a bit
uncomfortable by discussing it irreverently, saying, "I may well
start calling him the True Prophet. I haven't known so much verve

since I enjoyed the mighty *Shofar* horn of the False Prophet! Josephus! There's a lot of similarity there, and a lot of interesting contrast. One very long ago. One now. One a totally different exotic delight in being circumcised, one uncircumcised."

"I take it you are telling me that Josephus was one of your lovers?"

"An unforgettable lover, a man somehow in touch with the Beyond, in a way that I'm sure you yourself will be when you're older. And, sorry darling, there was an element in him that you or any other Roman could never match. And that element was the added seductiveness of being from a culture that is saturated with sexual repression. That element makes a man a real volcano!"

Offered Theophilus, "You really must write your sexual memoirs, my dear."

"Ha! I don't think that I could ever admit that I'd reached the point where I'm past doing and ready for writing! Was ever a woman as fated as I to lead a life of sensuality? Fated from the very start! Do you know where I got my name? I got my name from the festival called Floralia! In old Rome that festival of flowers was also a festival of sexual abandon. Every once in a while the old ways are revived by the adventurous, the curious, the outrageous. I was conceived during an orgy organized by Emperor Caligula during the festival of Floralia! That festival used to be even more raucous than Saturnalia! Actually, that reminds me that Saturnalia is taking place right now but I've grown bored with it that I don't even celebrate it anymore."

"Yes, people are out in the streets acting out every imaginable asininity, but I really don't care about Saturnalia anymore. It's just childish. Anyway, Saturnalia does retain a certain charm as a time of returning light and good cheer. I wish you *Bona Saturnalia*."

"*Bona Saturnalia*, to you too. I wish you good cheer, as Divine Janus brings in a new year!"

Theophilus searched his thoughts for what topic he wished to return to. "Yes, memoirs of yours would certainly start off in such a way that one couldn't put the scroll down. Caligula and Floralia! But I suppose your memoirs would be too scandalous for the decent citizens of Rome. People like Cato."

"Oh, you think so?" Floralia's look was wry.

"Cato is somewhat straitlaced, like the old philosopher Cato that he was nicknamed for."

"Think again! Cato may well like to tell people that he was nicknamed for a grand philosopher. But I know better! Cato means *cat*. You should have seen that fellow in the old days. Quite an alley cat was that one! Cato the philosopher indeed!"

"Well, I'll do without any salacious details about my friend," appealed Theophilus. "What I'd like to hear more about is the old Roman custom of combining spirituality with sexuality. One reads about how festivals such as Floralia and Lupercalia and Saturnalia used to be thoroughly orgiastic. And one reads about how combining spirituality and sexuality used to be common worldwide. But that sort of activity nowadays seems to be moribund, or at least very well hidden. What has happened?"

"We will indeed have a lot to talk about, you and I. But look. We've talked and shared amor till dawn. This is not the time to start a discussion on a whole new subject, I'm afraid. But I'll say this. Spirituality without sexuality is something like chariot races without chariots. Quite a sorry spectacle that. A lot of fuss and fuming and getting dragged around uselessly in the dust. Sheer frustration. No color. No hint of aliveness."

"Very amusing. Well, apropos of that, I'm sure that you'll be relating some incredible stories about Rome's past, and I'll be relating some incredible stories about the east."

Floralia gave her characteristic dismissive laugh. "Oh, yes, that trip to the east that you're planning. If that trip turns out not to be the dramatic revelation that you expect it to be, don't say I didn't warn you! All of that searching for a grand revelation here and there! Take with you on your journey a little quote from me and remember it always. I'll quote Luke as Luke quotes Jesus.

Jesus told the Pharisees that the Kingdom of God does not arrive with great signs of noise and portent, nor is it something that enables you to say, *There it comes!* or *'Here it is!* Instead… *Behold! The Kingdom of God is within you!"*

Theophilus now handled the little golden candelabrum around Floralia's neck and wondered a great deal about her; but he considered the hour too late for any more in-depth discussion.

She exclaimed, "Oh such a serious expression on that pretty young face of yours! Go your way now, dear philosopher Theophilus, and ponder and ponder and ponder!"

Then she said something that would truly make him ponder. "You will be swimming in much deeper waters, dear, than you even imagine. Well, that's exactly what you want. You crave that. Very well. Shall I help you drop into that awesome abyss? Go your way and philosophize on this. You have made love to a woman who long ago made love to the False Prophet mentioned in the *Book of Revelation* of the biblia. But far more has happened here. You have no idea what you have just done. Shall I tell you? Very well! You have made love to a woman who is a daughter of the Beast! Look at me carefully. Do you see it? Many claim that they can see it!"

Theophilus looked at her carefully in the dawn light and was stunned. Yes, he could see the resemblance! He could see the resemblance to that famous face of the monstrous beast that was to be found on innumerable discarded statues moldering away in disreputable places!

"Do you see it, my dear? The bloodline of the Beast?" Her chilling voice rumbled with primal force that had to be a matter of far more than two people's chance meeting to enjoy each other's bodies. Something rumbled. "Do you see it? My mother was sure of it! Absolutely sure of it! See it now! *I am a daughter of Caligula! I am the daughter of the Beast!"*

VII VISITING THE CATACOMBS

When the day came to attend a missa it turned out to be a "sun's day." Theophilus asked Cato about this as they descended into the earth on a rough stone stairway.

"It's another example of the Christians behaving like Jews yet not quite like Jews," explained Cato. "They observe a Sabbath day one day a week, but for them that day is the sun's day because that's supposed to have been the day on which Jesus was resurrected."

Along with a silent trickle of Christians, the men were entering a catacombs, an underground graveyard. Cato had indicated how fortunate they were to be able to witness worship services in this unique environment rather than in a private home. The scene certainly made for maximum reverence. On both sides of the passageway skeletons lay in eerie chambers. This was unlike a usual catacombs in which only the ashes of the poor found a final resting place. Cato explained that Christians shunned cremation because of their belief in bodily resurrection, and that very recently they had begun the practice of burying the dead in catacombs where all would await the resurrection together. Holding services for the living there helped further emphasize Christian togetherness.

Soon the handful of Christians and the two pantheists were sitting on benches in a dimly lit chamber waiting for the sun's day's service to begin. A bald man with a pleasant moonlike face stood before the congregation at a table and spoke a few words of greeting. Cato whispered that the man was named Clement and that he was one of the most notable of the Christians' "presbyters," or elders. Theophilus noticed that Clement was indeed an "elder" in that he was the only member of the congregation who looked to be advanced past middle age. Theophilus was thinking in terms of who here might be worth interviewing. The fact was, most of those present were women and most of the men looked likely to be slaves, groups whose credibility and powers of perception Theophilus dismissed out of hand. Clement would be the one with whom to speak. Then suddenly Theophilus noticed something extraordinary about the book Clement was now unrolling to read. Theophilus in his excitement pointed out his discovery to Cato in something more than a whisper, and Cato replied that they really should remain silent but would certainly take a close look at the book later.

Clement read to the assembly excerpts from a biography of Jesus that sounded to Theophilus similar to what he himself had already read, but not identical. Clement followed his reading with exhortations to the congregation to follow in their everyday lives the example provided by the text.

Next, he read aloud Paul's *Letter to the Hebrews* which, he explained, was addressed to God's new Hebrews, his new Chosen People, namely all those who lived in Christ. The passages had harsh words for fainthearted Christian backsliders. At one point the *Letter to the Hebrews* employed a metaphor depicting Christians as runners in a race towards a noble goal with a crowd of martyrs cheering them on. And Theophilus had to smile. Such was the spirit of the times: even religious fanatics were sports fans.

Theophilus listened intently to the *Letter to the Hebrews*. He wondered how much of it was going over the heads of the congregation. It was heady stuff, wherein God's *new Hebrews* were called upon to embrace a *new covenant* or *new testament*. The letter elucidated its points in a very arcane Greek. This letter seemed to represent that supremely mystical man Paul at his most genuine. Theophilus could see why learned people doubted the authenticity of Paul's supposed *Letter to Titus* and *Letter to Timothy*, letters which seemed to consist of a lot of petty complaining on the part of someone who wanted to raise his status among the Christians by pretending to be the voice of Paul. The *Letter to the Hebrews* was very much otherwise than those bogus letters. For all his intense training in Greek, Theophilus strained to comprehend the nuances. The letter maintained that Christ exists as an always-accessible sacramental presence, beyond time; and, being beyond time, *he speaks* the scripture continuously, and he is ever active though not present on Earth.

Presently the reading was concluded, and all rose, and Clement led the Christians in prayers for their worthiness of salvation. Those prayers were accompanied by the gesture of upturned palms held high near the shoulders, the *orans* position which was standard for prayer. Afterwards all exchanged a *kiss of peace*.

Theophilus was all along wondering why this ceremony was designated a missa, which connoted something being sent somewhere. He remained puzzled as assistants placed on Clement's table bread, wine, and water with which to dilute the wine. Clement proceeded to make a thanksgiving. He used the Greek word for giving of thanks, Eucharist, for these offerings of bread and wine. So there was a touch of Greek and there was also a touch of Hebrew. Those assembled had been taught at least one word of Hebrew, chiming in at appropriate places with a call of "amen." The bread and wine turned out to be representations of Christ's flesh and blood, which Christ had explained at his last supper he was offering as a sacrifice for all. At last came the explanation of the word missa: Clement declared he was sending up prayers and praise and thanks to God.

There remained only the lone segment of the ceremony in which Theophilus and Cato took part: the collection of alms for the poor. The Christians then dispersed as solemnly as they had gathered. Theophilus was anxious to take a look at Clement's book, but first he would have a word or two with Clement.

Clement beamed at his guests. "There you have it! A Christian meeting is hardly something that any man or state need fear but virtually a lesson in a school for piety!"

"We're very grateful for your invitation," said Cato. "We're both interested in knowing more about Christianity, but my friend here is especially keen on learning more about Jesus specifically."

"Oh?"

Theophilus explained, "I want to know more about what Jesus was like as a man."

Clement's genial face betrayed a trace of disconcertedness, but he tried gamely to be helpful. "Yes, it is important to remember that Jesus was a man. But also, that he was God!"

Theophilus inadvertently took a full step backward. Though hardly a religious person, he could not help but be stunned at the calm utterance of such a blasphemy. Still, there was nothing to do but steadfastly plow on and question Clement.

"Please, if we may, let's leave aside God for the moment and talk about the man. I'd be most grateful for anything that you can tell me that derives from witnesses to the life of Jesus."

"We are all witnesses to the life of Jesus." Clement seemed very pleased with the reassuring sentence that issued from his mouth.

"No. No. I'll try to be more specific. Have you ever spoken to anyone who actually knew Jesus?"

"My friend, that's the beauty of our belief in our savior! We all know Jesus! We have always all known Jesus!"

Theophilus felt he was engaged in a country dance wherein as soon as one partner put a foot forward the other pulled his own foot back, and the two could never touch. He pressed on.

"Sir, kindly tell me if you have any reminiscences of Paul when he was in Rome."

"Unfortunately, through my own foolishness I missed a golden opportunity for such priceless recollections. I had not yet seen the light when I was a young man and our blessed Paul and Peter were martyred. It was with the eyes of one blind, and from a distance, that I saw the blessed martyrs crucified on the Vatican, Peter among them."

Theophilus' interest perked up. He had never before heard anything about Peter being in Rome. This had the makings of a precious lead. Cato only smiled.

"Have you known people who knew Peter?" asked Theophilus excitedly.

"A transmission of *reminiscences*, as you would put it, never occurred, but instead a transmission of something far more precious." Clement held up his hands. "The apostles received a holy power directly from Jesus. I have been told that Peter laid his hands on a blessed martyr named Linus. Linus in turn laid his hands on a blessed martyr named Cletus, and Cletus in turn laid his hands on me. Dear friends, I'm not saying I can heal or work miracles as my blessed predecessors could, but something of the spirit, I feel, is there within me. I'm only a humble preacher, and I claim no precedence, but my brothers and sisters in Christ choose to show me honor because I am the only one remaining who received this priceless blessing from Cletus. No, I'm no Peter! We have elders, presbyters we call them, who see to our organization, but everything among us is extremely informal. Perhaps too much so when I find I have to remove presbyters who fall asleep too often during sermons! But I assure you something holy remains from the healing hands of Peter."

Clement excused himself to talk with some remaining members of his congregation.

Theophilus turned to Cato. "You never mentioned that Peter

was in Rome!"

"Yes, he's supposed to have died on Vatican Hill with all the others. There are other stories too. But I've talked with a lot of people, and I reached a firm conclusion long ago."

"And that is?"

"Peter in Rome is a fable."

Theophilus looked downcast. "But why should he become a fable?" he implored.

"He was the chief apostle, after all. Stories about him were bound to proliferate and get out of hand. But by all means make your own inquiries if you like. Just as you did here today."

"Ha! What a lot of smoke without fire! I don't know, Cato, I'm really beginning to wonder. If one can't get a straight story about what happened here thirty-five years ago, what chance do we have with events in Judea of twice that distance?"

"It's too early to get discouraged. Remember, Rome's community of Christians was always small, and it was subjected to the most brutal repression. Nero decimated the Christians and Domitian rounded up most of the ones who remained. A continuity of memories stretching far back simply isn't there. It'll be better in the east. The east is where the Christians are. Meanwhile, let's take a look at this curious book. Have you ever seen one like it?"

Theophilus approached Clement's table and touched his book. "I've seen smaller versions. Pharmacists sometimes have them. Who else? Librarians."

"Yes, this is the way to make a book for quick reference. They call it a codex. The Christians have made quite a number of them. They like to be able to find particular quotes from Jesus at a quick glance.

The codex was a book that to Theophilus hardly looked like a book at all. Instead of being a scroll it was a pile of rectangular pages which turned on a binding: exactly that which later ages would refer to, exclusively, as a book. He turned the pages curiously, and came to the conclusion that this might, in truth, be the coming thing.

"So, this is the *Gospel of Matthew*," he said, glancing at the first page, "the one by that tax-collector disciple of Jesus."

"Yes. Shall we read it through right now? Clement said he'd be glad if we did."

The literary adventurers soon realized that a codex had at least one disadvantage: two could not read simultaneously as comfortably as with a scroll. But they managed. Matthew's book opened with a dreary genealogy but soon improved. The story of the birth of Jesus proceeded much as in *Luke*, but with a few effective added touches, notably three gift-bearing wise men from the east and a guiding star.

"Pliny said a particularly noticeable star is a very ancient astrological sign announcing the advent of great riches," observed Cato. "And look here. In *Matthew* it's said, *Give him the name Jesus for he will save them from their sins.* Jesus is basically the Hebrew word for *he saves* or *savior.* And although not many people are aware of it, Jesus was also named Immanuel, *God is with us.*"

Less appealing to Theophilus than such niceties was Matthew's added narrative touch of King Herod's attempt to kill baby Jesus by killing all newborn Jewish males.

"As gruesome an incident as it is unbelievable," commented Theophilus. Why would anyone ever come up with such a thing? Barbarian tribes do such things to one another, but the Empire would never tolerate such an act on the part of a client king."

"Here's why the baby-slaughter has a place in scripture," claimed Cato. "That incident and many others are in *Matthew* as fulfillments of Torah prophecies." He proceeded to point out something outstandingly unique about Matthew. Incident after incident was followed by words such as "Thus was fulfilled the prophecy written in the scriptures," followed by the relevant scriptural quote. The Syrian rabbi's lessons would truly be helpful, thought Theophilus.

Cato continued, "Despite their problems with the Jews, the Christians tend to favor this one gospel which is the most Jewish. Here Jesus' life is, step by step, mostly a fulfillment of ancient prophecies from the Jewish holy books."

On went the story, notably *Luke*-like, but with an occasional glaring exception. At one point Jesus suddenly turned to the disciple Simon the fisherman and bestowed on him a new name, Peter, which meant *rock*, and gave him much, much more as well.

The passage had Jesus say, "And I tell you, you are Peter, and on this *Rock*, I will build my church, and the powers of death shall not prevail against it. I will give you the keys of the Kingdom of Heaven, and whatever you bind on earth shall be bound in heaven and whatever you loose on earth shall be loosed in heaven."

"I can't begin to explain that." Cato shook his head. Peter was seeming a more intriguing figure than ever. What was so special about Peter? When he attempted to emulate Jesus' walk on water he failed miserably. In Jesus' hour of need Peter denied knowing him. Yet everyone, apparently including Jesus, recognized Peter as the chief apostle.

The Christians' guests read the Christians' favorite book to the end, wherein the resurrected Jesus bade his followers to go and baptize all nations, and promised, "I am with you always, to the end of time." Then the two men closed the codex, thanked Clement, and set out on the short walk back to Rome.

Cato related a little tale on the road. "They say a most remarkable thing happened on this very road. Peter was trying to escape Rome, and suddenly he saw Jesus heading the other way, coming towards him. 'Quo vadis?' Peter called out to Jesus. 'Where are you going?' Jesus answered that he was going to Rome to be crucified a second time, seeing as Peter was too faint-hearted. This shamed Peter into going back to Rome. And there he was crucified, but upside-down at his own request because he didn't regard himself as worthy of dying in the same way as Christ."

"Peter always seems to be some sort of comical dupe, a

dramatic foil for the ever-perfect Jesus," observed Theophilus.

"Yes, at times you think you see before you a real human being with a real character. But then again there are endless numbers of outlandish stories that are obviously designed to pump up Peter's reputation as a miracle worker and Jesus' chief disciple. Some of them have found their way into some editions of Luke's *Acts* but are missing from others. That 'Quo vadis' story, by the way, is from an *Acts of Peter* that some Christians recognize as authentic, and some don't."

"I'm going to have to start making inquiries about Peter."

"Absolutely," agreed Cato, "and I'll bring you whatever literature I can find. Also, you really should read the *Gospel of Mark*. He was supposed to have been Peter's companion. The Mark gospel is supposed to be older than the others, but less complete, so it has lost popularity and copies of it are a little hard to come by."

"For my purposes it sounds crucial," said Theophilus. "And the older a copy I can find the better. I'll ask at shops that specialize in antique literature. The Sosii brothers I suppose would be the best."

"Yes, or try Atrectus near Caesar's Forum. Actually, though, I think Secundus is best. He's next to Vespasian's Temple of Peace. Secundus takes a personal interest in rare books, and in his customers' needs."

"I'll go talk to him."

"Good. And how are things going with the Syrian rabbi?"

"I like him better with each visit. He's been reading me the first part of the Torah himself. It's rather interesting, but there are twenty-two books in all. That's daunting in itself, but then the rabbi told me that to understand the books I'll have to read commentaries, and then commentaries on commentaries!"

Cato guffawed. "Commentaries on commentaries! Leave it to the Jews! They'll be analyzing and disputing till the end of time! But you're not discouraged, are you?"

"Quite the contrary! The unraveling of this mystery promises to provide some real spice to my life."

"Yes, it is rather exciting in its way."

"I'll make this journey, Cato. By now I wouldn't turn back if Jesus himself appeared before me on the road and demanded it!"

VIII DERIDING THE APOSTLE

On the next Jewish Sabbath, when Cato knew Theophilus could not be at the Syrian rabbi's, Cato paid call on Theophilus with an armload of books. He had not been at Theophilus' home before, and the second thing he noticed about it was that it was a most unprepossessing dwelling. The first thing he noticed, something that had most forcefully struck his eye, was a ragtag band of plebians lined up outside the door. Remarkable, thought Cato. Theophilus seemed to have adopted the rich Romans' custom of having clients attend him and fawn all over him in exchange for handouts every morning!

"Books on Peter, my friend!" declared Cato as Titus admitted him into Theophilus' presence.

"Witnesses to Peter, my friend!" said Theophilus as he rested his head on one hand at his table and with the other had indicated an old plebian who stood before him. He did not look happy.

"Go on with your story," he instructed the ragged man.

The fellow cleared his throat and expounded with heartfelt tones and gestures: "And there both of them were before Emperor Nero. Simon the Magician had failed. He had tried to fly but God struck him down and he fell in a heap at Nero's feet! But then suddenly with a 'whoosh' Simon Peter flew up into the sky, over the rooftops of Rome, soaring with the birds, over..."

"All right, thank you, that will be enough," Theophilus interrupted the man. Once given a coin, the man smiled and exited with a bow. "Titus, give the others outside a few coppers each and tell them they can go home," Theophilus told his slave. "And make sure you tell them I have all the information I need and won't be wanting anymore! Ever!"

Cato grinned. "So, you sent out a call far and wide for witnesses to the deeds of Peter!"

Theophilus nodded ruefully and Cato continued. "I'll wager you've had a valuable lesson this morning about whom to question, and especially how to question. If you offer money for information every loafer from here to the Tiber will come knocking on your door bearing a tall tale. What's more, your so-called witnesses all chatted with one another outside before they talked to you. I learned a thing or two during my years in law. Don't tell witnesses what you expect to hear, and don't reveal to them anything you've heard before. Talk to them subtly, and separately. Explore each witness's credibility with unrelated but telling questions. When you compare a collection of testimony skillfully, the truth tends to emerge most gratifyingly, much as a skilled glazier might watch clear glass emerge from a cooked glob of sand. For what happened today, of course, this is all irrelevant anyway. As I told you, Peter in Rome is a fable."

"That was the fourth time today I heard the Peter flying over Rome story."

Cato sat by Theophilus at the table and laid out his scrolls. "You'll find the story a number of times in these writings. For some reason there are endless tales of Simon Peter winning contests of magic over this Simon the Magician, a fellow who makes one appearance in *Acts*. I'm afraid you're not going to find much worthy of being taken seriously in all this rubbish. The *Acts of Peter* with the *Quo vadis* legend is actually the least inane of the lot. But I also have here a few things that are supposed to have been written by Peter himself. Here's *The Apocalypse of Peter*. As far as I know you've never seen an apocalypse before."

His curiosity piqued, Theophilus glanced through *The Apocalypse of Peter*. He read a portion aloud. "... And some there were there hanging by their tongues: and these were they that blasphemed. And under them was laid fire flaming and tormenting them. And there was a great lake full of flaming mire, wherein were certain men that turned away from righteousness; and angels, tormentors, were set over them. And there were also others, women, hanged by their hair above that mire which boiled up; and these were they which adorned themselves for adultery..."

Theophilus paused and made a face as though he had just swallowed vinegar. "This is absolute trash!"

"Well, it looks as though the apocalypse isn't going to be your favorite genre," allowed Cato. "Actually, *The Apocalypse of Peter* is even worse than you think. But as bad is it is, it's a strange fact that *The Apocalypse of Peter* contains the only example of humor that I've ever seen in any of the Christian scriptures."

"It must be humor horrible beyond all imagining."

"It is, actually. In *The Apocalypse of Peter* at one point Jesus is depicted high above in heaven, laughing at the fools on earth who thought they were beating and crucifying him. Such are the strange twists and turns taken by a variety of Christianity called Docetism. Docetists believe that Christ did not appear on earth in an earthly body, but only as some sport of disembodied spirit."

"Just trash, as I said."

"True enough. But here's something to be taken more seriously. The Christians treasure the letters sent by their holy men to their congregations. They use them for preaching. These two letters are supposedly by Peter. The *First Letter of Peter* and the *Second Letter of Peter*."

The letters being brief, they decided to read them immediately. In the first letter Peter seemed preachy indeed: *servants be submissive to your masters, wives be submissive to your husbands,* and *you that are younger be subject to the elders* were among his suggestions. Seemingly Peter had found it needful to remind a congregation to maintain the usual social norms in spite of the fact that *the end of all things is at hand.* The end of all things is at hand! Theophilus wondered how long the Christians would dare employ this letter in their services. Predicting an imminent end of the world was very risky indeed. He was also struck by the way that in this letter Peter, so mysteriously named *the rock* by Jesus, could not stop talking about rocks. All very strange.

"That letter may well have been written by Peter," said Cato, "but this second one supposedly by the fisherman is decidedly fishy. And not the least because the writer insists, 'This is now the second letter that I have written to you.' That insistence can't disguise the fact that the *Second Letter of Peter* is in a completely different style of Greek from the first. And look at this tremendously suspicious, ridiculous-sounding snippet."

The snippet read: "For we did not follow cleverly devised myths when we made known to you the power and coming of our Lord Jesus Christ, but we were eyewitnesses of his majesty."

Cato indicated another place in the text and said of it, "But here is the element that to my mind condemns this letter as a forgery with finality. See these? Passages excusing the delay in the end of the world that had been promised in the First letter of Peter! It's a common enough technique, trying to get your point across more forcefully by appropriating a great man's name. Many authors have appropriated Peter's name. Authors are driven men. If they can't achieve immortality one way they'll try another. In this case it's even been pointed out to me who the forger probably was. A fellow in the east named Jude wrote tracts making the same points as this letter, and in the same style. Read the *Letter of Jude* sometime and you'll see what I mean. Most likely this Jude fellow decided at some point that he'd make more headway in his campaign against the Gnostics if he appropriated the name of Peter. So he, Jude that is, wrote a letter under that illustrious assumed name, Peter."

"Gnostics? Those Egyptians, or what-have-you, who claim to have a special inner knowledge, a gnosis?"

"Yes, Christians who claim to have a special gnosis that they think sets them above all other Christians. And above all other human beings for that matter. We'll encounter them in the east. They all left Rome long ago. A strange breed, I hear, but reputedly guardians of a great many secrets."

"All of this keeps getting stranger and stranger," lamented Theophilus. "I hope and pray we stand a chance of clearing up the muddle."

"We do, rest assured! First of all, we can forget all about that nonsense of Peter having been in Rome. For one thing, there's Paul's *Letter to the Romans* which the Christians prize very highly. That letter starts with the usual salutations, and in this case gives salutations to around thirty Christians in Rome without mentioning Peter! The fact is, only very late and very foolish writings mention Peter having been in Rome. Drop him for the time being. So, have you spoken to Secundus yet?"

"Yes. You were right. He's very helpful. He promised to do his utmost to find for me the oldest possible copy of Mark's gospel."

"Splendid! Oh, and had you heard that Emperor Trajan is finally coming to Rome? He should be here by the next calends."

Theophilus nodded and maintained a bored expression. He had made up his mind not to be bowled over by the arrival in the world of yet another imperial *savior*.

Then Cato tried news that was more to Theophilus' liking. "I've arranged for my friend who knew Paul to receive you. You'll be visiting Lucius Livinius Piso, a man scrupulously honest, impartial, straightforward, and with an excellent memory."

Theophilus scrutinized the pile of Peter scrolls before him. "Cato, that will be... most refreshing!"

IX INTERVIEWING THE PATRICIAN

Theophilus read a copy of Paul's *Letter to the Romans* in preparation for his visit to Lucius Livinius Piso. The *Letter to the Romans* was an epistle widely circulated among Christians, as were all Paul's epistles, but this one was especially popular in Rome. And, sure enough, at the beginning of the letter there were thirty salutations to prominent Christians in Rome but no salutation to Peter. The letter was basically a summary of doctrine that Paul had sent ahead to Rome's Christians in advance of his visit to them. Paul's doctrine seemed to consist of an obsession with sin, in conjunction with the joyous conviction that Christ had provided the means to escape sin's ghastly consequences. Paul insisted that observing God's law was not the means to salvation; only Christ's grace brought salvation. To Theophilus, with his new knowledge of Torah, this debate could begin to be interesting. He saw that Paul had tried to inculcate in the Jews a whole new way of looking at God: not as a lawgiver but as a Father who saves "in Christ his son." No wonder the Jews had hated Paul! But what would say the gentile?

Theophilus arrived at the home of Lucius Livinius Piso. Though built on the same pattern as Cato's home, the place was larger and considerably more ornate. The owner was, after all, one of the few remainders of one of the most illustrious clans in Rome. When a slave opened the door Theophilus looked through to see the garden centerpiece that established the dominant theme of the house. It was a statue of a she-wolf suckling Romulus and Remus. Nothing could have been more illustrative of staid Roman respectability.

Theophilus was presented to Piso in his study, which appeared rather too large and too full of marble to be comfortable, Piso had the look of marble himself, and not only because his hair was as white as Cato's. Within his thin face a thin-lipped smile greeted Theophilus, and like a true lawyer of the old school he got down to business with a minimum of preliminaries.

"So, I understand you want to write a book about this Jesus and his followers such as Paul. You have there a fine idea, I'd say. The way rumors proliferate, and imagination runs wild, it's high time a believable bill of particulars was on file concerning the Christians, since we may not be rid of them as soon as some people seem to think. So, where to begin? I suppose as in a police report of the urban *vigiles*, with a physical description. Well, his real name was Saul, and as the nickname Paul implies, we're talking about an especially small man, very compact and intense. He was dark and sultry and bald, and somewhat ugly I'd say, with eyebrows that met in the middle of his furrowed forehead to give him a look of extreme intensity. His was an especially passionate and lively face that immediately attracted attention."

Theophilus was overjoyed at coming upon genuine details at last and was somewhat taken aback that Piso was describing a man who was in every particular the very opposite of Piso himself. Piso continued.

"I suppose you know how Paul came to Rome. He had originally intended to come to convert the whole city, thus making a good start on converting the entire world, but instead he arrived as a prisoner, and that after a shipwreck at Malta. But the fellow thrived on difficulties like that, that's what I think. He was

84

infatuated with this Jesus martyr and wanted to play the part of a martyr himself."

"Did you see him only in prison?"

"Not exactly. Paul was imprisoned but not really in prison. He was kept in custody at a rented house of his own choosing. One thing I'll say in the man's favor: although he was one of those wandering charlatans you see so many of, he did support himself. He was a tentmaker, and he worked at his loom making tents and awnings and tarpaulins right there in his home as he received visitors."

Theophilus had no difficulty picturing Paul's home. Poor folk all lived much the same, in a dark, cramped hovel with a bed mat, a few benches, a chest that served as a table, a number of clay jars, and an inadequate little charcoal brazier. He said, "It looks to me as though Paul's crime, whatever it was, was not taken very seriously."

"Well, do you want to know what his crime was? He was a renegade Jew who bickered with other more conventional Jews; that was his crime! But the little fanatic had the insane compulsion to be a martyr, as I said. He was in trouble with the Jews wherever he went throughout Rome's jurisdiction. That in itself couldn't have mattered less as far as Rome was concerned, but when violence resulted Rome had to step in. When the Jews brought Paul before the procurator Felix in Judea, Paul demanded that his case be tried by the emperor in Rome. And since Paul had Roman citizenship as a native of Tarsus, he had the right to make that demand. So Felix was obliged to send Paul to Rome, even though if the demand had not been made Paul would simply have been set free, just as he had been set free in many cities many times before. I fully agree with Felix who at the time told Paul he had gone mad from too much learning. Paul was learned, and clever... but mad."

"But surely Paul..."

"You think I exaggerate, young man?" Piso interrupted with a surprising tenor of emotion. "No, I don't exaggerate. Are you aware how Paul first discovered his Christ?"

"Christ appeared to him on the road to Damascus."

"Yes, a vision of Christ suddenly appeared to Paul on the road to Damascus, and it was as though Paul was hit by a flash of lightning. Paul suddenly converted from a fervent persecutor of Christians into a most fervent Christian. And why? Because of a flash of light that knocked him over, and a vision that followed. He told me the story himself and I was able to draw from the details of that famous vision-on-the-road-toDamascus story the obvious conclusion: Paul suffered from the falling disease. He was afflicted by the gods themselves. This turned out to be no idle guess on my part either. Others saw Paul undergoing seizures on several occasions, though I myself never did."

Theophilus felt a tingle in his veins. At last, he had a reliable witness who provided plausible explanations on matters of importance. Paul's sudden conversion to Christianity by encountering a vision of Jesus seemed to be explained by his having had a seizure caused by what was called "the falling disease."

Not one to tolerate ambiguity or a hint of rapture even for a moment, Piso continued in a tone that was almost excited. "So suspect is Paul's conversion story that, note this well, even in the Christians' own scriptures there are two completely different versions of the same event. One version has Paul's companions seeing what he sees but not hearing what he hears. The other version has Paul's companions hearing what he hears but not seeing what he sees!" Piso's facial expression betrayed decades of disgust at putting up with innumerable unreliable witnesses and bogus legal claims.

But exactly such matters were crucial to Theophilus' research. He probed his host's memory further. "Sir, I'm so very gratified that you're well versed in such matters. You must, then, have knowledge of the so-called *Book of Acts* by Luke. It purports to present a thorough history of the acts of Christ's disciples after

Christ's execution."

"History indeed. Young man, there's an enormous pitfall for you there. It might seem that the *Book of Acts* would be one of the best aids to your research, but it would actually be the very worst if you were to fall into that pitfall. That *Book of Acts* is not history but a novel. Surely by now you've found out that many widely variant version of the *Book of Acts* exist. And more versions are appearing all the time! And each and every version is chock-full of illogic and contradictions. All that the *Book of Acts* is, is the record of various factions within Christianity trying to shore up their own points of view by fabricating a history in which their particular hero wins victories for their particular point of view. The authors of the various versions of the *Book of Acts* occasionally succeed in following the standards of literature, as in following the custom of using the pronoun 'we' when relating sea voyages. However, to any trained Greek ear the whole farrago sounds utterly unhistorical. Every student of Greek has been through the rhetoric exercise of writing speeches to put in the mouths of famous personages. Didn't you do that exercise yourself as a student "of Greek?"

"Certainly."

"Well then, if you're familiar with that exercise you'll recognize that some author put speeches into the mouths of Peter and Paul and others, and the real giveaway is that all the speeches sound much the same. There's no real history there. Just monotonous speeches, all with the same tone and content. It's all just Luke, whoever he was, trying to make the point that all the acrimonious sects of Christianity should be in perfect accord because all of the early apostles supposedly were. But it hardly even matters what Luke was setting out to say. Because that original cartoon-like *Book of Acts* was interfered with, and added to, by later writers trying to make their various points. That deplorable *Book of Acts* is something like one huge theological graffiti wall!"

"How to get to the bottom of such a case under circumstances like that?"

Lucius Livinius Piso gave the barest hint of a chuckle. "It certainly won't be easy. Paul was a mystic and a man who reveled in being as mystical as possible. I'll speculate that Paul had another ailment that is characteristic of charlatans. It is called hypergraphia. This is an ailment under which a man has endless mystic visions and the accompanying urge to talk about them and write about them endlessly. Certain of Paul's weird ways are slightly hinted at in his writings. For instance, you must have heard the rumor that Paul castrated himself to demonstrate his thoroughgoing unworldliness and sinlessnesss. Many fanatics actually do that in the orient. There's evidence that Paul did so. The evidence is in his *Letter to the Corinthians*, where he declares that *natural* men tend towards un-spirituality, with *natural* men seemingly meaning uncastrated men. And in his *Letter to the Galatians*, he engages in a strange tirade against troublesome people who should castrate themselves. Then, a few passages later, he seems to proudly declare that he had himself castrated. *I bear the marks of Jesus.* This was one strange individual. He was a man nearly always unclear, with certain obsessions showing through."

Theophilus commented, "You seem to know so very much about this man Paul. Did you have a great deal of personal contact with him?"

"I played a minor role in a rather complex situation that revolved around Paul during his imprisonment. I was beginning a career in law and received an appointment as the assistant to an experienced lawyer who was assigned to Paul's case. Paul's case was to be considered an important test case. The state knew well who Paul was: the man responsible for spreading the Christian superstition outside the realm of Jewry. Among the Emperor's advisors, sentiment ran heavily in favor of executing him quickly. But there was a problem there. A martyr had been the cause of the whole wretched superstition in the first place. What horrors might come of having a second martyr? Besides, martyrdom was exactly what Paul wanted. I heard him rave on about its merits often enough. There was talk of eliminating the troublemaker Paul secretly. I would have had no part in any such disgrace, of course, but fortunately the issue never arose. Wiser heads prevailed. It was decided to proceed carefully with Paul, to treat him with circumspection and merely keep him under observation for the time being."

Theophilus reacted visibly to this statement.

"You look surprised, young man," continued Piso, "but Roman law is not all flogging and crucifixion. Find a more humane rule of law than Roman law somewhere in the world if you can, or a law that has better assured equity or public order! I know we're talking about the reign of the monster Nero, but we're talking about the first five years of Nero, the quinquennium, when his rule was mild and praiseworthy. During the quinquennium Nero still listened to his advisors, worthy men like Seneca, who kept Paul alive and well. Naturally there was never any chance of Paul gaining an audience with Nero, though that was Paul's ostensible reason for being in Rome. No, no purpose could have been served by presenting the madman epileptic to the madman spoiled child posing as Emperor. Instead, Paul was merely kept under observation."

"And he was free to meet with his own people, correct? Luke said so."

"Yes, this Luke was careful to say so, no doubt, to emphasize that Paul was considered no threat to the state. And at the time that was indeed true. So, Paul was free to receive his bickering Jewish friends and together they bickered the day away."

"Were you in attendance with Paul for whole days at a time?" inquired Theophilus.

"No, but I was with him for extended periods, at times. My role as assistant to the counselor assigned to Paul's case consisted largely of notetaking. I addressed Paul rarely, but I heard all. The little fanatic would expound on his fanaticism without pause if we'd let him. Ah, he was a showman, that fellow. He loved a show to such an extent that, runt though he was, he salted his speech with athletic metaphors. *I have run the good race. I have fought the good fight.* A real glutton for attention was he. He'd wave his arms about and bellow, *Everyone should share my ecstasy in Christ; except for my chains I wish to God that everyone could be exactly like me!*"

"*Chains*, you say?"

"A typical self-serving exaggerated turn of phrase for the martyr-to-be. There were no chains."

"What did Paul say about Christ, especially about Christ as a living human being?"

"That was an odd thing. Yes, that was odd. Paul talked about Christ repeatedly, but never, absolutely never, not once, did he speak in a manner that would lead you to think that Christ had been a living man. Paul talked about Christ as though he were some kind of god that followed him around, and a most mysterious god at that. It was always 'Christ is in you' or 'You are in Christ' or some such mumbo-jumbo. I thought at such times we were close to finding out something about the very basis of the whole superstition, so I made a point of asking Paul, over and over, to tell us something about Christ's actual life as a man. Always he evaded such queries with mysterious doubletalk."

Theophilus stirred in his seat. The tale was uncannily like his own experience with Clement. He had reached the very heart of what he had hoped to learn from Piso, but several questions remained. "What happened to Paul ultimately?"

"Yes, how to get rid of Paul 'ultimately,' but quietly, that was the problem faced by the Roman state. Ultimately even a vacillating official has to decide what to do with a problem. And what would many an official do with many a problem? Then, as now, as always? Why, pass it on to another official, of course! The responsible official took advantage of a statutory limit that decreed the release of a prisoner after two years if no witnesses against him had by then appeared. Paul had always harped on how anxious he was to head west to preach. In the end he was issued a writ of relegatio, a temporary exile to one's place of choice. And off he sailed to Spain. Off sailed the problem, to a place sufficiently large and sufficiently distant to make us think we'd seen the last of him."

"Had you seen the last of him?"

"To everyone's misfortune, no. As I understand it, Paul's mission to Spain was a failure, something that Christians sometimes reluctantly mention but would rather not say much about. Out west people think differently than in the illogical east where Paul had been so popular. From Spain he returned to Rome, driven by that irrepressible martyr syndrome of his, I have no doubt. The situation here had changed enormously in his absence. No more quinquennium. No more reasonable Nero. Nero had kicked his pregnant wife to death and had murdered his mother as well. Thousands of others would follow these first two victims to Hades, and obviously a man like Paul stood little chance amidst such circumstances. It was the eighth year of Nero. A new treason law had been enacted."

"Paul was executed?"

"As quickly and as quietly as possible, outside the city. And without speeches. He was firmly gagged and bound. Roman citizenship gave him the right to a beheading, and a beheading had the added advantage of precluding any nonsense about some magical resurrection of his body. When the swordsman did his work a very definitely separated and unresurrectable Paul-head was displayed to the few witnesses present, including myself. The Christians have always liked to say that Paul's head spurted milk when he was beheaded. I could get any number of women, slaves, and laborers to swear to that this very day, even without the application of judicial torture." The thin-lipped smile was not appealing. "But Paul's head spurted blood. Just blood. And that reminds me of how much that strange man had always loved to talk about blood. Christ's blood. Spilled blood. Offered blood. Salvific blood. Blood, blood, blood."

"Why was Paul so obsessed with blood? Could it have something to do with his initial conversion, when he was struck by a vision of a blood-soaked Christ while on the road to Damascus, a city whose very name means *blood*?"

Piso sighed. "I certainly don't know the answer to that. Paul's bloodlust probably had everything to do with his martyrdom obsession that I've outlined. Paul spent his last days dictating his *Letter to the Philippians*, a work which really oozed with the attitudes of a man who was perfectly content to be facing martyrdom. Phrases like, *The peace that passes all understanding.* And, *Be innocent children of God, shining as lights in a perverse generation.* Phrases like that."

"I'd appreciate anything you can tell me about the members of Paul's entourage," requested Theophilus. "Barnabas, Timothy, Luke, Linus, Titus."

"They came and went. Any of them who were leaders were likely to have been executed around the same time as Paul. Paul's scribe was named Tertius. I was informed that Paul dictated all of his letters to Tertius, with a few exceptions. Paul wrote by hand one of his least important letters, his *Letter to the Colossians*. Let's see now, what else can I recall? Paul's usual missionary traveling companion Timothy, who had a Jewish mother and grandmother and a Greek father, from Asia Minor. Another of his companions, Titus from Antioch, was not Jewish. The one follower of Paul's that stood out in my mind was the woman. Paul lived and traveled with a woman named Thecla. They were said to live chastely as brother and sister."

"Really? I never heard anything about that."

"Nonetheless I can guarantee you that it was so. She was an oddity and was therefore quite memorable. She dressed in men's clothes and she preached. I don't have to tell you how many reasons later Christian writers would have for leaving Thecla out of Paul's story! By the way, there's an accurate description of Paul's physical appearance in a book called the *Acts of Paul and Thecla*. Paul is described there as small and bald, and robust and charismatic, with crooked legs, and with eyebrows that met. And though I can't vouch for it, he's also described as sometimes taking on the looks of an angel."

Theophilus nodded. So many surprises seemed to be in store. He found himself wondering whether he would eventually discover that Jesus himself had a wife. It was remarkable to what extent opinions could differ on so basic a matter. Most said that Jesus never married. But some said that he married Mary Magdalene. And some said that he married someone named Sophia. But he broke off his daydream when he realized that Piso was relating more information at a rapid clip.

"Now then, I was talking about the time when Nero tore into the Christians. Nero's eighth year was a turning point. His savagery broke loose in full fury. Everyone lived in fear. My own family was decimated. My friends died or disappeared or turned into enemies. It need hardly be surprising that at the time I gave no thought at all to what was happening to the squabbling Jews. But one thing I do remember. One other case was considered as important as Paul's, and that individual was executed at approximately the same time. That man was Paul's rival Mark."

Theophilus' eyes widened and his mouth fell open to exclaim, "Mark was in Rome!"

"I don't know how much time he spent in Rome, if any. He was a wandering preacher like Paul. I do know that he was executed in Egypt, fed to the lions. For prominent rabblerousing religious fanatics, that was favored as a method of execution that doesn't leave many leftovers for the superstitious to concoct resurrection legends about." Theophilus avoided looking at the thin smile this time. "Mark did have a following. The only other thing I can tell you about him is that Paul occasionally made disparaging comments about him. Here was one renegade Jew criticizing another renegade Jew for not being the right kind of renegade Jew, and naturally I could not make head nor tail out of his ravings. I only remember that he called Mark *kolobodaktylos* and that it wasn't meant kindly as his own nickname was."

"*Kolobodaktylos*? Stump-fingered?"

"Yes."

"But why?"

"I haven't the faintest idea."

"Mark was supposed to be a companion of Peter. Do you have any recollections on Peter?"

"He's no more than a name to me. A Christian holy man, second only to Christ himself, I think. Strangely enough, I'm quite sure I never heard of him until after the night of the living torches on Vatican Hill. Then the legend took hold that Peter had been one of the Vatican 'martyrs.' I got the feeling that Peter was an ever-growing legend."

"Are you so certain that Peter's execution on Vatican Hill was a legend?"

"Yes, and I'll tell you why. You may or may not be aware that the events on Witches' Hill, which is to say Vatican Hill, were grounded on the Cornelian Law Concerning Assassins and Poisoners. It prescribed crucifixion or death by wild animals for convicted magicians and prescribed that arsonists should be burned alive. All those punishments took place that night on Vatican Hill, all for the purpose of deflecting from Nero the accusation that he had purposely set fire to Rome. The effect was indeed memorable, but not in the way Nero had intended. All that was impressed indelibly on everyone's mind was the unlimitedness of Nero's bestiality.

"What is all too easily forgotten is that other elements of society suffered even greater depredations at the hands of the Beast Nero. Yes, everyone took to calling him *the Beast*, and that name made it into the Christians' *Book of Revelation*, as a synonym for the worst-possible earthly evildoer. We older families of Rome were nearly wiped out completely. Nero feared our authority and was eager to confiscate our wealth. But only the Christians lived on in the popular memory as victims of Nero, and they made the most of this false memory. So, one need not be amazed that they would fabricate the tale that Christ's greatest disciple Peter met his end at the hands of the world's greatest beast, and in the most dramatic imaginable way.

"I'll only add that the only law of Nero's that was not rescinded after his overthrow was the Institutum Neronianum, the anti-Christian legislation. Thus, it would seem that Christians are the most persecuted inhabitants of the Empire, but actual numbers speak otherwise. Christians constantly lay claim to an honored place among those persecuted by the accursed Domitian, but the fact was that the Christians' own customary persecutors were among those that Domitian most persecuted: id est officialdom, nobility, the well-placed and successful; anyone likely to arouse that miserable monster's envy."

No, thought Theophilus, no one was free of the tendency to see all from their own prejudiced perspective; certainly not this aristocratic lawyer. However, he had been an invaluable witness, certainly the best yet. New tales, images, opinions, problems were buzzing in Theophilus' brain as he made his way home. That night, inevitably, the preacher Paul and the prosecutor Piso were in his dreams.

He dreamed of an eerily lit basilica, a court of Roman law. The scene was familiar to any Roman: a magistrate presided over legal proceedings sitting at the end of the basilica, high within a semicircular apse with an altar to the gods before him. Lucius Livinius Piso was the magistrate. Before him stood the accused Paul, holding high his chains as he pleaded his case not to Piso but to the Almighty. Paul was known to have appeared in several such scenes in reality. Suddenly, however, occurred a turnaround of a most extraordinary nature. Lucius Livinius Piso, so smug in his magistrate's chair, his cathedra, was transformed slowly into the whitest marble, then crumbled to dust and disappeared. Then Paul broke his chains, ascended to the altar, sat in the cathedra, and was master of the basilica. Theophilus consulted every book of dreams he could locate but found no explanation remotely relevant to his weird vision.

X SECURING THE SCROLL

Theophilus was in a bit of a hurry through Vespasian's Forum, but stopped when something caught his eye. A series of reliefs that he had seen often enough before had taken on added interest. The reliefs showed the emperor performing religious rituals accompanied by his courtiers, and also by quite imaginary beings who were mixed in liberally with the courtiers. Victory was there, as were Fortune, Plenty, and Rome herself, all anthropomorphic goddesses mixing most amiably with the humans. Theophilus wondered if anybody in the distant future might have to wrack his brains to sort them all out, much as he was wracking his brains to sort out Peter, Paul, Luke, Mark and Jesus.

He was hurrying to follow a lead concerning *Mark*. Secundus the bookseller had just discovered the oldest copy of Mark's gospel that he had ever seen. It dated clear back to Claudius' reign or earlier, to judge from the look of the handwriting and the papyrus. The owner was a Christian who was quite willing to sell, according to Secundus, who was willing to facilitate such a deal as a favor to a steady customer. Mark's gospel was much shorter and less complete than Matthew's, in addition to not being written by an eyewitness, so that it was not much in favor among Christians. The owner of this Mark had indicated he would like to have a brand-new *Matthew* in exchange for his antique Mark papyrus, So a brand new *Matthew* was precisely what Theophilus now carried under his arm. He arrived in the right neighborhood, not a bad one at all. The Christian in question was a tradesman in comfortable circumstances. Theophilus knocked on the tradesman's door, with a stout kick as was customary, and a tall man answered the door and greeted him with a friendly smile.

"You're Theophilus? Well, I thought you'd likely send a slave rather than come yourself! You're most welcome! Come in!" The man motioned Theophilus over to a table where the yellowed Mark manuscript lay waiting. "As a Christian I regarded the notion of accepting money for this book as somewhat unseemly, but Secundus suggested the perfect solution: an exchange of two texts that will satisfy both of us owners. When at first I objected that my worn-out *Mark* could hardly equal a new *Matthew* in value, he explained that its very age gives the book an added value, and is the very reason you're interested in it."

"Exactly so," agreed Theophilus as he handed the tradesman his freshly inked *Matthew*. "I trust you'll find this satisfactory."

"Many thanks. Yes, we sometimes hold prayer meetings here, and we've been hoping to get hold of a *Matthew*. I'm almost ashamed of this sad old scroll I'm giving you. It's really falling apart, but Secundus said that that's fine."

"It's exactly what I need," said Theophilus, inspecting the scroll. "The older the better."

"Well, I suppose I'll miss *Mark*, but let's face it, it's not the fine work that *Luke* or *Matthew* is. A rough style. A lot missing. And everything that's in *Mark* is in *Matthew* anyway. So we can do without it. But I'm certainly pleased it will be in good hands."

Theophilus placed the scrolls side by side. "*Mark* certainly is much smaller. You say there's nothing in *Mark* that's not in Matthew?"

"Or at least nearly nothing. And... Well, I don't know if this is of any interest to you, but since you took the trouble to come here yourself..." The man took out a wax tablet on which he had scratched some notes. "Since I knew I was going to give up *Mark*, who served me well, I jotted down those passages which, as well as I could ascertain, are the only ones that are unique to *Mark*."

"Yes, I'm very interested in that! Thank you so much for showing me that!"

"Well then, let me copy them down for you on another tablet."

"I'd be most grateful."

"All right then, let's see. There's the part where people claim Jesus is insane and his family denies it. Rather unflattering to our savior; best left out. Then there's a parable of a seed growing of itself. Not so bad, I suppose, but what's the point? And, let's see, Jesus heals a deaf man with his spit and a blind man with his spit. No, I don't like that at all. Then in a parable about salt Jesus says, 'Have salt in yourselves and be at peace with one another.' No one seems to be able to figure that out. Lastly, when Jesus is arrested one of his followers escapes the soldiers by darting off and leaving his loincloth in their hands. Some say that that was a personal reminiscence by Mark about something that actually happened to him. But who knows?"

"Who indeed? Well, thanks again, and enjoy your Matthew." Theophilus took up his tablet full of notes and his scroll to leave, and unrolled the scroll a little to read a bit of his new possession. It was rolled to the text's end, as was usually the case. He took a few steps, reading casually, then suddenly stopped dead in his tracks, profoundly disconcerted.

"Is something wrong?" asked the tradesman.

"No, no! I'm only surprised at this ending of the scroll, that's all. You've seen it, of course."

"Ah that. Yes, I'm sorry about that."

"This ending of *Mark's* is nothing like the other gospel endings at all! Three women find Jesus' tomb empty. Very well. They see a young man in a white robe sitting there. Very well. But then!"

The rest of the ending of this *Mark* scroll read:

And he said to them, "Do not be amazed. You seek Jesus of Nazareth, who was crucified. He has risen, he is not here; see the place where they laid him. But go, tell his disciples and Peter that he is going before you to Galilee; there you will see him, as he told you." And they went out and fled from the tomb; for trembling and astonishment had come upon them; and they said nothing to anyone, for they were afraid.

"No one interacting with a resurrected Jesus. No ascent to heaven. Nothing but three frightened women running from an empty tomb! They claim that there is a risen Jesus, but no one even sees him!" exclaimed Theophilus.

"Oh, it's not like that at all!" proclaimed the tradesman. "But I'm extremely sorry about selling you damaged goods. What happened is obviously that the original ending fell off some early copy. The last sheet of papyrus must have come unglued at the end of the roll."

"It would be unprecedented for such a damaged scroll to be copied. And without a title? The title of a book is almost always on the last sheet." This was indeed the case. Human nature being what it was, scrolls were almost always left for the next reader to re-roll, and because of that the titles were placed at the end. "And what Christian would copy such a thing? What is Christianity without Jesus' resurrection?"

Assured the tradesman, "All the more reason I think the whole thing is a mistake. You see, the text really cannot have ended here, right in the middle of a sentence at the word *gar*. A Greek sentence can't end with *gar*!"

"I'm afraid I disagree."

"Well, doubtless your Greek is better than mine. I... I don't know. As a tradesman I'm hopeful that I haven't sold you damaged goods, but as a Christian, well of course I hope to Jesus that I have!"

Theophilus hoped he had not upset the man and put a friendly hand on his shoulder. "You've given me something very precious, my friend, and such giving was, if I'm not mistaken, Jesus' explicit instruction: 'It is more blessed to give than to receive.'" He would have lingered to try to make his consoling more complete, but he simply had to rush off to show his find to Cato.

Cato turned out to be interested, but, rather irritatingly, claimed to have a piece of news that was superior. "You remember how I told you Emperor Trajan was about to arrive in Rome?" Cato even sounded as though he thought that that mattered.

"Yes, and I hope that the wonderful news you have for me is not that Trajan has promised to build the world's greatest library in Rome, because I've already heard." To Theophilus' mind, saviors tended to be all things to all people. Caligula and Nero and Domitian may very well have made the very same promise, and many other promises that reassured people that they would turn out to be wonderful rulers.

"It's not that, Theophilus. Listen. I will be able to get us an audience with Trajan!"

Theophilus was speechless. This was a shade more unexpected than even the ending of *Mark*.

"We'll only exchange a few words with the man, but, nonetheless, what an occasion! Well, I need say no more. I've seen the imperial palace before, but you're in for quite a treat! Though I dare say you don't seem to have much taste for luxurious accommodations!"

"You could have tried a little harder to disguise your distaste at my lodgings!" laughed Theophilus. "But lodgings are expensive in Rome. Why spend a fortune for luxury? I'd rather spend the money on books."

"You know, Theophilus, the fact is we should be spending all that wasted rent money on books. Why don't you come live at my house? You have only that one slave. It wouldn't be a problem at all. And we need the books!"

Within days the move was made, and the books were

purchased. Cato and Theophilus happily applied themselves to the task of spreading out scrolls in Cato's library and comparing the texts. After *Matthew* and *Mark* and *Luke* had all been rolled out beside one another for weeks, the two scholars concluded that most of *Mark's* material appeared in *Luke* and nearly all of that material was also to be found in Matthew. Conversely, all that was unique to *Mark* were a few odd or incomprehensible or unsavory passages, some of which the tradesman had pointed out to Theophilus. *Mark's* Greek was simple and unprofessional. *Matthew's* was better and *Luke's* was far better still. *Mark's* manner of expression was disordered and clumsy. *Matthew* and *Luke* smoothed out *Mark's* problematic sections, improved the cumbersome and perplexing and removed the potentially offensive. When all was said and done, no doubt remained that *Mark* had been written first. In addition to using *Mark*, the other two gospel writers had apparently used some other source not available to Mark, and that was a matter of major interest, but for now all the researchers' attention became focused on *Mark*, that being unquestionably the earliest available sourcebook on the life of Jesus.

At one point Cato burrowed in his library alone with *Mark* for a day and came out to show a pile of wax tablet notes to Theophilus. "I believe that *Mark* has confirmed, with the evidence in his writings, the rumors about his association with Italy. It struck me as odd that *Mark* used the Roman army method of dividing a night into four watches. Of course, any Jew might happen to know about that, I suppose, but look here. *Mark* talks about a hypothetical woman who commits adultery by divorcing her husband in order to marry another man. But a woman divorcing a man!? That's pure Roman law, something quite out of the question under Jewish law! And look at this. I don't know how often he got them wrong, but *Mark* very often pauses to explain Jewish customs to his readers. So who was he talking to? Who were his readers? Certainly not to the Jews of Judea! Here he explains the meaning of the word Golgotha, *the place of the skull* where Jesus was crucified. All that is interesting enough, but one passage all by itself dispels any doubt in my mind that Mark wrote in the west. He said that the widow's tiny contribution to the Temple was a quadrans. That coin is the deciding piece of evidence in my court. The quadrans was at all times used only in the west!"

In order to investigate Mark's gospel further, Cato and Theophilus obtained some newer copies. A claim that had been made by the Syrian rabbi quickly proved to be cogent. Christian copyists did not tend to transmit a work unaltered. "Here begins the gospel of Jesus Christ," began all copies of *Mark* simply. But then some copies added the designation *the Son of God*. Was it really so easy to turn a person into a Son of God? Another addition reflecting a point of view later than Mark's own was, *The time is fulfilled, and the Kingdom of God is at hand; repent and believe in the gospels.*

But of all the many instances of tampering to which *Mark's* opus had been subjected, the now infamous ending was far and away the most significant. Cato compared the various attempts at fleshing out *Mark's* original abrupt termination and shook his head. "Where exactly lies our *corpus delicti*?" intoned the retired lawyer. "We have a crime here. Embellishment. Forgery. Misrepresentation. And, well, lying. It's up to us to solve this crime, and find the perpetrators, and the victims, and... the truth!"

XI BEHOLDING THE GOD

Cato and Theophilus ascended to a place where gods dwelled. Accompanied by a retinue of attendants they climbed the Palatine Hill, the site of the imperial palace, the source of the word *palace* itself. Of Rome's seven hills only the nearby Capitoline Hill was higher. Only Jupiter himself was higher than the emperor. The Capitoline Hill was crowned by the Temple of Jupiter, a stupendous burst of white marble ornamented with splashes of gold. Cato pointed out where Caligula had constructed a bridge connecting his own home with Jupiter's so that the great gods could commiserate with each other in private.

The Palatine overlooked the Forum on one side; and, crossing to the other side of the hill, Theophilus knew the view would be equally spectacular. Suddenly it came into view: the Circus Maximus, the chariot racecourse that accommodated a full quarter of a million spectators. The emperor and his people had a god-like vista of the Circus, while, from below, the Palatine had the appearance of a home for the gods.

Now, inside, Theophilus saw the full grandeur of the god home that very few mere mortals would ever see. White and gold were the customary colors of heavenly architecture, and here that hue of heavenly architecture was complemented by the white and gold livery of innumerable slaves and attendants. Marble, polished woodwork, fountains and rare plants were everywhere, but the outstanding feature that most insistently struck the eye was arches. Arches lined up with arches and were piled upon rows of other arches. Arches were the Roman structure par excellence and the emperors seemed to have built as though they could never have enough of them.

Cato was familiar with the layout of the palace. He indicated where Augustus had lived in a relatively modest home in an era when the rest of the Palatine was inhabited by other wealthy families. Subsequent emperors had taken over the entire hill, with Nero even extending his grandiose building plans down into much of the land by the Forum, including the site that his successors later used for the Colosseum. Domitian had fairly recently built on the most lavish scale of all, even providing himself with a private racecourse for future visitors such as Theophilus to gaze upon in awe.

This is the corridor where Domitian was stabbed to death," indicated Cato at one point.

"But no monument like the one that Julius Caesar got at his stabbing site," remarked Theophilus, "and, worse than that, there's not even a monument to the stabbers!"

Cato glared at him. "Times may have changed but some things don't change at all. You'd better be a little more careful about what you say while you're here."

"I'm sorry. Anyway, I'll keep scrupulously to your instructions about what to do in the emperor's presence: say nothing unless asked a direct question."

"Exactly right."

Cato and Theophilus were ushered into the imperial audience chamber, a place which was for them nothing astounding after having already been satiated with wonders. Nor were the jostling clumps of middle-aged men there anything special. Emperor Trajan himself was differentiated from them only by his being seated and by the royal purple on his toga.

Theophilus' first view of an emperor close-up gave him new respect for Rome's artists. Trajan looked exactly like his statues: a stern soldierly expression under a distinctive straight hairline. This man was everywhere being called *optimus*, "the best." Theophilus had heard all about the funds distributed to needy children, the clement decrees and pronouncements, and the promises of a great library. Yet he had also heard of Nero's quinquennium, and he wondered how long any man with a horde of courtiers fawning on him night and day could remain *optimus* in fact as well as in name.

Attendants introduced prominent and less-than-prominent Romans to Trajan and he exchanged banalities with them. Trajan tried politely and unsuccessfully not to seem bored. The afternoon wore on. Flies invited themselves to the audience, and to Theophilus their buzzing mixed indistinguishably with the rest of the proceedings.

Cato was an old man being obliged to stand for a long time, since no one sat in the presence of the emperor on such an occasion. Theophilus could see strain on his friend's face and pitied him, as he had when he had first seen him as a stranger straining to read. He looked around at the other faces in the room and they turned out to be quite a study. Some were bored or strained like the faces of Theophilus and Cato. But others ran the gamut, from nervous, to scheming, to fawning, to mellow.

Suddenly, though, Theophilus' study was interrupted as his own name was announced and his literary ambitions were described. To his intense gratification, Trajan actually appeared to perk up and take interest.

The emperor did indeed seem to be a humane man. Despite his reputation as a pure warrior, he made an effort to speak in tones that were not overbearing. "Young man, I applaud your intention to investigate the fundamental causes of Christianity. This inquiry should prove most helpful. I am determined to leave Christians in peace as long as they themselves keep the peace. For now, I don't know if that will be an interim solution or a permanent solution. What is necessary is to come to understand what makes anti-social superstitions like Christianity popular in the first place, so that such superstitions can be pulled out root and branch."

"Most assuredly, Dominus," said Theophilus, having properly spoken when spoken to."

Trajan then speechified, "I mean to govern very much in the tradition of the Divine Augustus. He was a man and a god who realized that governance is useless without attending to the ethical fundament of society." There followed an imperial soliloquy on the breakdown of morals in Roman society.

The soliloquy became an extensive one, and despite the fact that the Emperor of Rome was addressing him directly, Theophilus believed his eyes were glazing over. Speeches of this nature were a sore point with Theophilus. Nothing was more common in Rome than old bores who would sit together the whole day long and drone on and on, decrying the demise of the old Roman virtues.

The audience had by now gone on for quite a long time. Theophilus noticed that some others were bored by the imperial soliloquy. This was a certainty because Theophilus noticed, to his surprise, that some of them were daring to whisper to one another. His natural inclination was for his attention to fly, like a bee to pollen, to whatever factual minutiae were the most captivating at the moment. And therein lay his dangerous mistake. He let Trajan's too-familiar speech fade into the background as he tried to hear what some of the courtiers were daring to whisper.

Theophilus vaguely heard Trajan say something about his own efficacy as Emperor being judged more for his ability to provide bread and circuses, which were a moral low, than for any solid achievements. Then all at once Theophilus realized he had been asked a direct question by the Emperor! Somewhere in the drone there had appeared a question, that was directed, with an unmistakable gaze, directly at Theophilus! But he had not been paying adequate attention! Feeling as though his heart had fallen into his stomach he struggled with all his might to remember what the question had been!

"Rome is always having its latest trends, and I'm afraid they're a mystery to me. Who was that writer anyway?" That was Trajan's question. A kind whisperer standing behind Theophilus saved him. He prompted Theophilus with the missed imperial question. Theophilus hastened to mumble apologetically that he too was a newcomer unfamiliar with the fashions in Rome, and so knew little about the latest fashionable writers.

Trajan then threw out the question to the whole assembly. It was Cato who came up with the answer. "Juvenal is the writer in question, Dominus. It was Juvenal who coined that phrase that has become such a catch-phrase, *bread and circuses*."

"Ah, Juvenal, yes." The emperor nodded. "Some silly epigrams, but some fine ones too. 'Bread and circuses,' he said, that fellow Juvenal. Very much to the point. Satire can be exactly the refreshment one needs at times. At its best it teaches us how to live our lives better. Rome can do with that." Again, the imperial soliloquy led up to a question for Theophilus. Trajan wanted to know what appeal there was in a superstition like Christianity. And he seemed earnestly to want to know. His look of boredom had disappeared. Theophilus, determined to do better this time, fell back on his hard-earned skill at rhetoric, and addressed his Emperor.

"Dominus, to you or me an evangelion from a distant land, a misty dream replete with hollow promises may be a spring too shallow to offer us drink. But as for women and slaves, what else do they have in their lives but dreams? And I think that question is more urgent still as regards the urban poor, all the thousands who have been uprooted from their agrarian culture and have come to live in the cities of our great Empire. The old gods don't follow them easily down those narrow alleyways that they must now call home."

All were silent. Theophilus was afraid he might have been too blunt. Surely, rare was the occasion when anyone present had had an inclination to think about the sort of people he had just mentioned, much less do anything for them. But Emperor Trajan continued the discussion in a way that indicated approval of Theophilus' statements. Then he motioned for a young, bearded man standing near him to come closer so that the two of them could discuss something privately.

A beard was a great rarity among Rome's elite. A beard made a definite statement. Theophilus realized at once that the man with the beard must be Trajan's nephew and assumed heir Hadrian. Gossip being the Roman staple that it was, Theophilus had heard a great deal about Hadrian. People called him the *Greekling*. Hadrian was known to be infatuated with Greek philosophy. Hence the philosopher's beard, which Theophilus regarded as the apex of pretentiousness, especially on a man so young. Theophilus wanted to think well of everybody, but he had trouble doing so with Hadrian, especially when he had heard so many times that the *Greekling* could not keep his hands off little boys.

"Well, good Theophilus," intoned the great Trajan, "it seems my nephew has some degree of interest in an idea that suddenly occurred to me. He has always wanted to travel east to see the sights. With such an interesting and erudite traveling companion as yourself available, this may be the perfect time!"

Theophilus felt a creeping nausea in his gut. The unrefusable offer of an unwanted traveling companion seemed likely to ruin the trip on which he had his heart set. Hadrian now made a little speech which did not make Theophilus feel any better. Inspired to talk about Greece, Hadrian spoke in mediocre Greek with an annoying Spanish accent. He entertained the company with two quotes from Euripides, one of which he made a hash of, while the other he enunciated well enough, but it was not really from Euripides at all! Theophilus tried not to grimace. What could a journey be like with the *Greekling* along? He would have to pretend that every idiotic literary misquotation was a gem! What desperate deed might he have to perform to escape? Feign illness? Jump off a ship? Marry?

Imperial uncle's and imperial nephew's further whispered conference seemed to be inconclusive. Trajan again addressed Theophilus. "Well, we'll let that matter rest for now. I think there are a few ways I can assist your interesting project. First of all, I'll provide you with letters indicating my interest and approval. And in the letters, I'll indicate that you have my permission to use the imperial post if that should prove helpful to you. All I ask in return is that you post me a letter regarding your progress from time to time. And, for whatever it's worth, you have my permission to explore the imperial archives. You're probably aware that at least three thousand inscribed tablets went up in flames in the archives during the post-Nero civil war. But I hope that whatever is left might be of some use to you."

Stares were being directed at Theophilus, some of admiration, some of wonderment, some of envy. The god known as Emperor Trajan had showered favor on him. The treatment he encountered in Rome would be considerably different from now on.

Once they were far away from any ears related to the palace, Cato asked Theophilus what his impression of Trajan had been.

"In every way positive," he replied. "But we'll only really know in twenty years."

"We!" Cato laughed heartily. "You'll know, maybe, but certainly not me! And by then you'll probably know all you need to know about Hadrian as a ruler as well!"

"I pray that he has a long apprenticeship!"

"My boy, you'll never make a courtier. Your lack of regard for Hadrian was eminently clear. I'm flattered, but rather surprised, that you want to have me along with you on your journey but not someone like Hadrian who is your own age."

"How old is he?"

"Twenty-two."

"Then he's a few years younger than me. But age isn't the

point. We'd be a traveling court if Hadrian came along. I'm sure I don't care for life at court."

"His presence would certainly alter the tenor of the journey," agreed Cato, "whether for good or ill it's impossible to say. Anyway, I highly doubt that Hadrian will be indulging in anything as petty as scholarly travel anytime soon. Rumor has it that Trajan is about to prepare one of the largest military campaigns of all time. He wants to conquer Dacia."

"Dacia. Dacia. Every emperor wants to leave his mark on the world through conquest. But now they're apparently scraping the bottom of the barrel. Only the leftover lands still remain ripe for conquest! Ridiculous Nero held a big party in Rome for the client king of Armenia and declared that he had thereby conquered Armenia, but in fact he was the one who lost Armenia! Hmm. Dacia! A land even more remote and more dreary and more unimportant than Emperor Claudius's Britain!"

Cato shook his head. "No, actually I've read about Dacia, and it turns out to be quite large and tremendously fertile. And the land even has a surprisingly superior culture, complete with a network of paved roads. The talk is that the Dacian land will suffice to reward retired Legionnaires for many generations to come, constructing out of that land a real Nova Roma."

"It's odd that there's anything of interest there in Dacia at all, since it's just north of Thrace which nobody thinks well of. Some lands seem to be under a curse, and Thrace is one of those. The Black Sea, also known as the Unfriendly Sea. Ovid's horrible place of exile. Horrible witches. Horrible warriors. Horrible Spartacus."

Cato enjoyed any opening to discuss history. "Yes, Spartacus. Our Roman heroes always love to prove themselves by defeating a larger-than-life villain. A Roman hero conquers Numidia by defeating Jugurtha. A Roman hero conquers Asia by defeating Mithridates. When Trajan conquers Dacia, he will be defeating a certain Decebalus, whose name announces that he is as mighty as ten warriors!"

Theophilus spread his arms out wide to lean out over a marble balcony and survey the majesty of Rome that was spread out before him, all in the manner of a Roman conqueror. "So where does that all end, all of that very Roman spirit of conquest? You die, miserable, at the age of 33, and you order your people to parade your body through the streets with hands stretched out empty to show that you die possessing nothing."

"Alexander."

"Yes," nodded Theophilus. "What's the point, in the end? Alexander conquered the Persians, and we don't know if even Trajan can match that scale of conquest. Then even if you conquer the Persians, and weep like Alexander because there are no more worlds to conquer, then what? One can't really conquer the whole world. They say that India is every bit as large as the entire Roman Empire. And so is the Land of Silk."

It was Cato's turn to nod. "The world is indeed large. They say that south of Egypt there stretch lands even more vast than the places you've just mentioned. Lands so vast in their extent southward that they're even canopied by stars different from our own."

Visions of exotic places filled Theophilus's head. And those visions aroused ruminations of the strangest nature. "Look out over our proud Rome. For some reason, lately, our wondrous city keeps reminding me of something, and never more so than during this visit to the imperial palace. I keep getting reminded of how the Devil tempted Jesus with an offer of *all the kingdoms of the world.* You'd have to say that rejecting that offer was the crucial decision in the man's life! All else followed. And now as I look out over Rome from a mighty height, for the first time I'm reminded of something from the *Book of Revelation.* In that book, our dear seven-hilled Rome is depicted as a horrendous beastly dragon with seven horns!"

"Hercules! Much food for thought there," murmured Cato. "But enough. It's time to remove ourselves from the palatial

Palatine and do what we're made for, namely our studies. We're scholars, not conquerors."

"And at the Imperial Archives no less! I take it that that's a very rare honor."

"To say the least."

"Yes, Trajan was exceptionally helpful. Let's hope that that will be the case with the rest of the gods as well!"

XII CONSULTING THE ARCHIVE

7he state archives occupied a site whose prestige could hardly be surpassed: next to the Jupiter Temple on the Capitoline Hill. The high and lonely location had in itself something to say about Rome's archives: they were important, yet they were unimportant. State documents were expected to be used only once, then shut sway and stored near temples, as a sort of pile of holy talismans that somehow symbolized the continuity and sanctity of the state. Rummaging through the talismans to put them to actual use was an infrequent and difficult matter, but Theophilus was prepared to try.

Theophilus was taken on a tour of the archives and was aghast. This Roman holy shrine was truly a mess, almost as bad, in its own way, as that holy of holies on the other side of the hill, the Temple of Moneta where, all too often, shamefully debased coinage had been minted. The archive's scrolls and tablets were kept piled to the ceiling in room after room, vaguely labeled but with no attempt at indexing. Some documents on related subjects were pasted together chronologically or in alphabetical order, while others moldered along with companions, related or unrelated, in trunks. Theophilus saw that the only hope he had in this Augean stable was to disburse some enormous tips, some of the best coinage that the monetary goddess Moneta had to offer.

The ploy worked wonders. Soon attendants were scurrying to and fro to find Theophilus old documents on Judea. Cushions, too, appeared like magic, and he settled down to reconstruct a somewhat familiar saga from brittle pages that told the story firsthand.

King Herod had been Augustus' brutal but effective tool for keeping order in the ever-rebellious province of the Jews, Judea. Evidence for Herod's crimes was massive; missing, however, was any evidence for the incredible story of the slaying of the infants mentioned by the *Gospel of Matthew*. Herod's death caused the country to be administratively partitioned and allowed pent-up tensions to flare. The worst disorders occurred when pilgrims flooded into Jerusalem during festivals. Then the Roman procurator would march in with his troops from Caesarea to watch over matters from the Fortress Antonia, which adjoined the Jews' Temple. When Pontius Pilate was procurator, he seemed to enjoy taunting the Jews just as much as he could, notably by minting coins with pagan symbols and by bringing legionary standards into Jerusalem. His unauthorized use of Temple funds to build an aqueduct almost resulted in his recall, but the actual recall came sometime later as a result of a run-in with the Samaritans over the purported arrival of the Samaritan messiah. In Rome, Pilate's trial for misuse of office petered out in a welter of dreary legal documents.

Judea was a very special province, at once especially rich and especially troublesome. Herod was an inveterate builder who provided the province with a marvelous up-to-date Roman-style infrastructure, including the capital Caesarea, which was a supreme flattery to all the Caesars and was also the world's first artificial port. A good port for Judea was necessary because the country specialized in the manufacture of luxury goods. These included dates, figs, balms, ointments, perfumes, and the like. They were exported to every corner of the empire, and money poured back into Judea. Jewish festivals in Jerusalem brought in still more wealth from all over the empire, via the pockets of pilgrims. The population reached a million. But even with prosperity in place the Jews chafed under Roman rule to a greater degree than almost any other people in the empire, so that political trouble was always brewing anew.

Roman power in Judea came to the verge of collapse when Caligula announced his intention to place a statue of himself in the Jerusalem Temple. Only his sudden death averted war. Then Emperor Claudius' friend and client King of Judea, Herod Agrippa, managed to keep the peace for a few years. Interestingly for the Jesus case, there were records of prophets who preached imminent upheaval and were merely flogged. But after Herod Agrippa's death the upheaval did come. The documents told a doleful tale of a land where zealots, brigands and professional dagger-men terrorized decent citizens into emigrating in droves.

Those who emigrated early from Judea turned out to have been the lucky ones. The troubles came to a head in Caesarea when some Greek youths, egged on by Nero's blatant favoritism in recent local disputes, taunted the Jews by sacrificing a cock in front of their synagogue on the Sabbath. The silly incident mushroomed into a political tumult that eventually led to the Jerusalem Temple priests' suspension of sacrifices to the emperor. And that insult to the emperor amounted to a declaration of war.

The crisis in Judea led directly to Nero's downfall and his falling on his sword. Thousands of others perished in considerably more horrible ways: butchered by soldiers, crucified, starved. The most capable general in the Empire, Vespasian, was enlisted to conduct a campaign of mass terror against the Jews of Judea, all the Jews of Judea whether rebels or not. And with this all-important victory to his credit, he won laurels as the new Emperor. His son Titus fought the campaign in Judea to the bitter end, at the siege of Jerusalem. Titus' triumphal arch, depicting the parading through Rome of the treasures of the Temple, was to be seen in the Forum not far away. Now, thirty years after that victory, much of

Judea was still a wasteland. Jews were scattered worldwide, and a special Fiscus Judaicus required that all the tribute they had once paid to their Temple now be paid towards the upkeep of temples of Jupiter.

By and by, Theophilus held something very special in his hands. It was a brief letter, and a trite letter, but a letter composed by Pontius Pilate himself. He was tempted to embezzle the precious document away, but the possible punishment for such an act was too daunting; all his plans would then be likely to crumble, just as surely as would every yellowed papyrus in the state archives. Theophilus put Pilate's letter aside with a sigh. He did write down a wax tablet copy of it, this brief letter about increasing difficulties with the Samaritans that aptly illustrated Pilate's hot temper. This document was likely to be the best item he would ever find here. Far too much had indeed gone up in flames. He rose to leave. With so much else to keep him busy he decided that he would hire someone to try to find whatever else remained to be found here. Some starving poet or rhetorician would be overjoyed to be handed such a cozy winter job. Theophilus would meanwhile remain free to enjoy the less lofty and less musty pursuits that Rome had to offer in abundance.

XIII WINNOWING THE DETAILS

*N*o more evidence concerning Pontius Pilate ever turned up at the archives. Nor would Theophilus and Cato find out anything more of interest in Rome about Pilate, Mark, or, infamously by now, Peter. They did, however, carry out other worthwhile research throughout the winter. One day Cato came to Theophilus carrying a pile of tablets. The look on his face was that of a lawyer who was certain that he had just successfully compiled the research that would prove his case.

He announced, "You'll be amazed at what I've found, my friend. I've compiled a list of the sayings of Jesus that indisputably pre-date him. This is a list of the sayings of Jesus that the rabbis assure me were widely known in Jewish literature *before Jesus*."

Cato read the sayings out. They were:

Why do you notice the speck that is in your brother's eye but not the log that is in your own?

Anyone who looks at a woman lustfully has already committed adultery with her in his heart.

Ask, and it will be given to you. Seek, and you will find. Knock, and it will be opened to you.

Be as wise as serpents and as innocent as doves.

The Sabbath is made for man, not man for the Sabbath.

*Unless you become like a little child you will never enter the
    Kingdom of Heaven.*

Love your enemies and pray for those who persecute you.

And there were others, but Theophilus believed that he had
gotten the idea, and hardly listened as Cato droned on with more.

When Cato had finished, he said, "I found this notion of Jesus
using nothing but old tried-and-true saying so intriguing that I
searched my own memory for more examples, not from Jewish
literature but from Greek and Roman literature. And, sure enough!
Most of the rest of Jesus' sayings came precisely from there!"

Theophilus resolved to spare himself another long recital of
sayings, so he asked if he could simply skim this list himself. He
read the following sayings attributed to Jesus, which Cato had
paired with their earlier origin among Greeks or Romans.

"Blessed are the poor, for theirs is the Kingdom of God."
Jesus... "Only the person who has despised wealth is worthy
of God." Seneca.

*"If someone slaps you on the cheek, offer him the other
also."* Jesus... "Practice putting up with being abused,
refusing to get cross at insults. You'll be able to go on from
that to taking a slap and saying to yourself, 'I seem to have got
entangled with a statue.'" Roman philosophers.

"Treat others as you would have them treat you." Jesus...
"Take care not to harm others, so others won't harm you."
Seneca.

"Seek and you shall find." Jesus... "Seek and you shall
find." Roman philosophers.

*"It is like a grain of mustard seed which a man took and
sowed in his garden. It grew and became a tree, and the birds
of the air made nests in its branches."* Jesus... "These words
should be scattered like seeds. However small a seed is, once
it's in suitable ground its potential unfolds, and from
something tiny it spreads out to its maximum size." Seneca.

"Be merciful, even as your Father is merciful. Judge not,

lest you too be judged." Jesus… "Someone asked how he could master himself. Diogenes replied, 'By rigorously reproaching yourself with what you reproach others with.'" Stobaeus.

"*Can a blind man lead a blind man? Will they not both fall into a pit?*" Jesus… "Some people prefer to be provided with a blind guide rather than a sighted one. They're bound to take a tumble." Philo.

"*Consider the ravens. They neither sow nor reap nor gather grain into barns, and God feeds them. Are you not worth more than the birds? And why worry about clothing? Consider the lilies of the field, how they grow. They neither toil nor spin. Yet I tell you even Solomon in all his finery was not arrayed as one of these.*" Jesus… "Why not consider the beasts and the birds and see how much more painlessly they live than humans do, how much more pleasantly and healthily." Dio.

Added Cato, "And plenty of Greek philosophers have said, *Seek and you shall find,* just as Jesus did. And haven't we done just that, sought and found? Jesus also said, *Nothing is hidden that will not one day be made known or a secret that will not eventually come to light,* and that saying has been repeated through the ages by any number of philosophers and is something that should hearten us on our quest today!"

Said Theophilus, "Maybe so, but your lists certainly demolish any claims that Jesus might have had to originality. So a real mystery arises. What was the man's appeal? Was it his rhetorical flourish?"

"Ah, who is to say? We've only just begun to learn anything about the man. Maybe it was indeed his rhetorical flourish. Or his way of explaining. Or his political persuasiveness. Or his mere presence. Or maybe it was the miracles after all."

"The one big miracle would have been enough: the rising from the dead. But the oldest copies of the oldest gospel, *Mark's,* certainly cast doubt on that having happened. How desperately we need to be in the east! How desperately we need to speak to people who actually knew the man!"

"True. All too true." Cato pondered. "But what can we usefully do while we're still here in Rome? Hmm. I do believe I know what I want to investigate next. It seems to me Mark is the key. Surely Mark is the key. Mark's is the oldest gospel. The one that later authors depended on and simply embellished." Back went Cato into his lair, with the announcement that he was going to plunge into a further understanding of the question of the intentions and reliability of Mark.

Many days later Cato emerged to make his pronouncements. They were not propitious. The main problem was that the Mark gospel had been tampered with by so many later hands that it came close to uselessness as a piece of literary evidence. And even the original pristine version of *Mark*, as far as it could be ascertained, often seemed to be just one huge headache for a researcher.

Clumsy Mark! Shoddy Mark! Stump-fingered Mark! His Greek was atrocious, his style puerile. His Greek sounded artificial, as though episodes were clumsily patched together without any narrative logic. *Then this… then this…* Sometimes anecdotes were unskillfully patched together topically. Sometimes otherwise-unrelated sayings were strung together by catchwords. The *Mark* text bore all the hallmarks of a rickety attempt to concoct a narrative out of many disparate anecdotes and sayings. Mark's Greek had an unnatural fairy-tale feel, the feel of a story that had not taken place in any particular real location at all. Jesus appeared in *the wilderness* or on *the mountain* or in *the house.*

In *Mark*, examples of inept narrative abounded. The phrase *And passing along by the Sea of Galilee he saw Simon and Andrew* seemed to have been taken from an earlier episode stating, *And passing along he saw Simon and Andrew*, to which Mark had added the words, *by the sea of Galilee*. This stitching-together was apparent because the Greek syntax was so poor. For the phrase *passing along* was not customarily followed by the word *by*. In other words, the setting of the Sea of Galilee had been added at a later stage by a later hand to give the story some color. So spoke the linguistic evidence.

Was the Sea of Galilee just some vague romantic eastern setting for *Mark*, who was a man of the west, in other words the Latin-speaking western half of the Roman Empire? Cato and Theophilus reviewed instances of Mark's unfamiliarity with Judea that they had gone over before. There were always more instances to find. Mark wrote for an audience so remote from Judea that at one point he explained, "The Pharisees and the Jews in general never eat without the hands."

But the eager researchers proceeded far beyond such trivialities. They wanted to get to the nub of the question: Who did Mark believe that Jesus was? The world's earliest known mention of Jesus as the Son of God occurred at the very beginning of the *Gospel of Mark*, which intoned, "The beginning of the gospel of Jesus Christ the Son of God." The problem was that many manuscripts of *Mark* omitted the words "the Son of God," altogether, making it almost certain that in the original version Mark's gospel began, in Mark's usual clumsy way, with the simple words, *The beginning of the gospel of Jesus Christ.* Yet, to complicate matters, perhaps Mark did indeed believe that Jesus was the Son of God. In the crucifixion scene he had the sympathetic centurion say, *Surely this was the Son of God.*

Unfortunately, the centurion could just as easily be understood to have expressed a much milder, *Surely this was a son of God!*

"Surely this was a disparity in meanings of earthshaking proportions!" joked Cato at one point. Indeed, if Jesus had been regarded as simply a son of God, then that really meant very little. Numerous people were figuratively regarded as a son of God in the Jewish scriptures, beginning with Adam.

Theophilus and Cato paid much regard to a supremely important passage in the gospel of *Mark*. It was a passage which confirmed Jesus as either the Son of God or a son of God. The passage was the only place in the entire Christian canon in which God spoke! The fact that there was only one place in the entire Christian canon in which God spoke was itself puzzling. During Jesus' baptism the heavens opened, and the Holy Spirit descended in the form of a dove and God said, "You are my beloved son, in whom I am well pleased." The text was quite unclear as to whether Jesus was the only one present who heard God's voice; thus it was unclear which of two very different situations held true.

Luke repeated this story of God speaking during Jesus' baptism, and in the oldest texts of Luke God then quoted a psalm and said, "You are my son, today I have begotten you." The trouble was that the actual Greek phrase connoted God's *adoption of a special person*, as had always been common among Jewish prophets. There was no hint of a divine *only-begotten son*. At this point in Mark's gospel the divine spirit entered Jesus. That incident brought up the next topic. For if the divine spirit entered Jesus *only at a certain point*, then there could be no question about Jesus himself being God!

Some researchers referred to the primitive Mark gospel as *the gospel in which Jesus was not Christ*. In *Mark*, there was a Jesus, but there was not yet a Christ. After all, Mark had Jesus say, "My God, my God, why have you forsaken me?" Theophilus discussed this utterance and concluded that these were hardly words to be uttered by a divine Son of God, much less words to be uttered by God himself! This was a most curious, if not to say outrageous, belief held by some Christians: this belief that Jesus was himself God.

Theophilus and Cato were satisfied that amidst a literary windstorm of confusion they were at least able to put that bit of nonsense to rest. They discovered that the earliest mentions of Jesus as God were to be found in two Christian books that were almost universally regarded as being both very late and very spurious. Those books were the *Letter to Titus* which purported to be by Paul but was obviously not by Paul, and the *Second Letter of Peter*, which purported to be by Peter but was obviously not by Peter.

And in *Mark*, at one point, a man called Jesus "good master," and Jesus said, "Why do you call me good? There is only one who is good: God alone." This was a fairly explicit statement by Jesus himself that he was not God. Indeed, wondered the researchers, if Jesus were God why would he have needed to be baptized? Such a baptism would have been a case of: "Who doing what to whom, and why?"

The researchers found that dozens of times in the Christian scriptures Jesus was "declared to be" or "preached as" or "believed to be" or "called" the Son of God. But Jesus himself was coy when asked if that was who he was, the Son of God, and he uttered phrases such as "You have said it." In contrast, there were about twice as many mentions of Jesus being the Son of Man, and they were usually his own mentions. To put it plainly: Jesus often called himself the Son of Man and never called himself the Son of God. That was an exceedingly odd topic to be left aside for future study.

Who was Jesus? Clue after clue arose, only to be squelched. Luke began his gospel with an elegant prologue, and followed that up shortly thereafter with a phrase that had the ring of history, on the model of Herodotus and Thucydides and Polybius: "In the fifteenth year of the reign of Tiberius Caesar…" But in between that prologue and that phrase someone had injected an episode in amateurish Greek that did not seem to be Luke's at all. It was an episode that was apparently intended to demonstrate that John the Baptist was subordinate to Jesus from birth. Joh the Baptist seemed very intriguing, but almost nothing was known about him in Rome. Here again was a matter that seemed to require investigation in the east.

There did seem to exist one clear clue about John the Baptist. The later the gospel the more Jesus was made to appear superior to John the Baptist. Cato and Theophilus heard tell of a recent *Gospel of John* in which Jesus was the Light, while John the Baptist had merely come to bear witness to the Light and therefore hailed Jesus with a series of messianic and divine titles.

These investigators often dedicated late nights to their studies. One day Theophilus saw that Cato's eyes were discolored with sleeplessness. But the man seemed satisfied with his night's work because his eyes also glowed with the verve of a lawyer who was working on the case of a lifetime. He summarized, "What we may have here, in all of this Jesus mania, may be a case of extreme embellishment of the life of Jesus in order to make him seem superior to that contemporary rival prophet, John the Baptist. There are quite a few rumors that there live highly spiritual people in the east who are lukewarm about Jesus but worship John! The last of the Jews' holy books, Malachi, ends with a prophecy about the return of Elijah: 'Behold, I will send you Elijah the prophet before the great and terrible day of the Lord comes.' Then Mark's book seems to endeavor to take up where the saga left off, by beginning with John the Baptist who is regarded as a return of Elijah. Mark certainly felt that he had something important to say: the obvious continuation of the Jewish scriptures that ended with Malachi prophesying a return of Elijah! We'll certainly have to be looking into this John the Baptist. Then there's the added perplexity that there is a cult following of a quite distinct figure who is also named John. That's the John who was supposedly Jesus' favorite apostle, and who also wrote the most mysterious gospel about Jesus, and who also wrote a phantasmagorical apocalyptic climax to the biblia, namely the Book of Revelation. Rumors. Rumors. We really must get to the east to really find out! This is beginning to be exciting!"

XIV ENJOYING THE GRACES

𝒯heophilus lived with Cato, conducted research with Cato, and attended social occasions with Cato. How droll it was, then, to run into the old man one day at the entrance to a public privy. Moreover, Cato was excited about something and would not let Theophilus go on his way. The man lived for books and lists, and lists and books, thought Theophilus. At this moment he was carrying armfuls of both and insisted that they needed to talk immediately.

So, odd as it seemed, they went together into the privy to sit down and have their talk. Rome was well provided with these large public facilities. They were a crying necessity in the world's only super-city, as well as a significant source of state income because of the small coin that was demanded for entry, by the hundreds of thousands. As Vespasian once famously told Titus: coins derived from the latrines did not smell any different from other coins. The privy consisted of a long stone bench running around all four inner walls, the bench being equipped with holes to accommodate the seated users. Privacy was neither a Latin word nor a viable Roman concept.

Said Cato, "We're leaving on our adventure so very soon. I've been determined to settle this Peter thing once and for all before we leave. It's all so strange. Various legends associate Peter with Rome, but the most sober testimony always cries out that no such person ever lived here. Now, Peter's writings allegedly consist of two important letters, but these so-called *First Letter of Peter* and *Second Letter of Peter* are utterly ridiculous drivel. Rather than making Peter come alive the two letters actually make him seem even more legendary. Here's a queer thing. 'Peter' means 'stone.' And the *First Letter of Peter* cannot stop talking about stones! Listen to this. *'Come to him, to that living stone.' 'Behold I am laying in Zion a stone.' 'The very stone which the builders rejected.' 'A stone that will make men stumble, a rock that will make them fall.'*

"The *Second Letter of Peter* is a real travesty, a completely failed attempt to concoct a sagacious letter in the tradition of Paul. It even resorts to ending the earth's existence in a loud noise and a consuming fire! It's an attempt at high drama, but it's really low farce. And this pitiful work is the earliest work ever to claim that Jesus was God! And here's the most ludicrous part of all: the highly suspicious statement, *For we did not follow cleverly devised myths when we made known to you the power and coming of our Lord Jesus Christ, but we were eyewitnesses of his majesty.*"

Asked Theophilus, "So are these supposed letters of Peter bogus enough and useless enough to just them leave here in the privy?"

The answer was no, but the various sounds echoing through the facility certainly lent the documents an even less dignified air than Cato had attributed to them. Cato continued. "I've made many inquiries and I think I may be onto Peter's trail. I think I can begin to understand how this chief apostle of Jesus who was named Simon was transformed into a legendary figure named Peter. It all has to do with the Vatican. The verb *vaticanare* means *to prognosticate.* As you know, the Vatican is connected etymologically with witches and witchcraft, and historically the place was always crawling with witches and witchcraft. Well, it turns out that there has been taking place a battle to lay claim to the sacred caverns underneath the Vatican. So our answer to many mysteries has to do with a struggle in the depths and bowels of Rome."

Theophilus could not but guffaw at this point. The image, whether intentional or accidental, was simply too coincident with the noisy activities in this meeting place of many Romans. However, Cato spoke on in utmost earnestness.

"You're aware how the cult of Mithras always meets in caverns. There is a Temple of Mithras deep down underneath the Vatican. Mithras was a god who was so very similar to Jesus. He was a bearer of light, born on the twenty-fifth day of December, whose birth was witnessed by shepherds and by Magi who bore gifts. He performed miracles and cures and ascended to heaven. Christians have been trying to lay claim to this extremely powerful Temple of Mithras beneath the Vatican, along with many of its traditions. Now listen to this. The Mithraic god of that place is called Pater Patrum, *the father of fathers*. How easily is the name Peter derived from that figure. And that figure is also sometimes called *Papa*. Mithraism is not terribly ancient. Mithraism itself usurped the Vatican caves from some other cults not so very long ago. The original god of that place was called Attis. Attis means *father*, in other words: Papa! The place positively reeks of the worship of an ancient father god! And in this place's sanctum sanctorum there stands a sacred phallic stone! What else? It's so obvious! A lot is revealed now. A sacred phallic stone is called a *peter*!"

The gods certainly had their strange, mocking ways, thought Theophilus. What a setting in which to be discussing reeking and peters! In spite of the absurdity of the setting he had a feeling that this conversation had been vital. Everything about the conversation pointed to one person with whom further discussion would be profitable: Floralia. He had been visiting her occasionally and was eager to be off to visit her once again right now.

The gods surely were in a mood for laughter this day. Theophilus arrived at Floralia's house at a juncture that seemed like a scene from a comedy. She was just bidding goodbye to two huge gladiators. Covered in perspiration and exuding excitement, she greeted Theophilus merrily.

He tried to excuse himself. "I'm sorry. I seem to have come at a most inopportune time."

"On the contrary, my beautiful young scholar, I think the gods had a hand in sending you at the perfect time! Those two dear beefy fellows are just meat, after all. You and I together, on the other hand, are meat with spice! Let the appetizers depart and let the main meal begin! Oh, where are my manners? I should at least ask. Would you like me to call the gladiators back?"

"No thank you, Floralia. That's not the nature of my appetite."

"I know just the thing then." She snapped her fingers and called out, and two young slave girls arrived." I recently purchased these two girls who were marketed as a pair. That dark Nubian beauty is called South, and that golden-haired lovely from the German lands is called North. Clever marketing, no? Let me show you how well they've been trained as bath attendants. And so on."

Floralia slipped into her steaming bath and let out an "Ah!" of ecstasy and was the perfect picture of Roman luxurious indulgence. North and South rubbed her down with oils, and she called out, to Theophilus, "You are of course invited to join me."

Once Theophilus did so, and was enjoying his portion of the slaves' rubdown, he began to wonder why he had ever considered leaving Rome. But at length he did recall that he had, after all, a mission. Sipping a delightfully strong wine, he recounted Cato's tale and asked for Floralia's opinion. The wine was indeed a strong one, and she answered volubly and with somewhat misplaced glee.

"You want to know all about the strange goings-on at the Vatican, do you? Well, you have come to the only person in Rome who can really tell you! Because those who are actually involved with the strange goings-on will never tell any outsider the truth!

Unless… and this is the really big 'unless'… unless they are boasting to a woman in bed! That is, a woman in bed who is curious about such matters and wants to know more. And that's why I know the truth! Even though I've never been in the Vatican caves. I've squeezed the truth out of many a man who has!"

She paused to drink a good deal more of this day's wine, which seemed strangely unlike any wine that Theophilus had ever had before. He pondered how nice it would be to be able to afford such wine. He believed that the main additive was something called opium, from Asia Minor.

"You know, Theophilus, how little boys always seem to come up with the idea of a clubhouse that's only for boys. The girls are derided and excluded. That's what the Vatican has become, but on a larger scale. It was always the sacred center of Rome, exuding a strong spiritual power. Witches' terrain. In ancient times the realm of spirit contact was more a women's realm than men's, but that has gradually been changing. And nowhere has the change been more notable than at the Vatican."

More wine.

And more of the intoxicating story poured forth.

"Quite recently there appeared the world's only all-male religion, Mithraism. It seemed natural for the Mithrans to take over the Vatican, and they did so. The Vatican depths were always inhabited by the most masculine of gods: the city's patron god Pater Liber, *the Almighty Father*. That god also bears a name that is common in other parts of the world: Attis, *Father*. Or: *Papa*. And, as is common in other parts of the world, his shrine is a phallic stone located somewhere deep inside the Vatican."

"I'm conversant with all of this," interrupted Theophilus. I've been discussing it with Cato."

"Yes, there have been times when I've discussed it with him too, over wine and phallus." She giggled like a girl, something which Theophilus had never heard before and which she seemed to greatly enjoy. She slapped his hand and chided, "All right, there's bound to be some repetition, but just relax and let me tell my story, playmate!

"Somewhere there in the Vatican, the mysterious secret phallic worship takes place, worship of all that is male. You will be surprised, and yet perhaps not surprised at all, to hear that the sacred stone is called Peter. Peter the Rock! Ha! Of course! Like other phallic stones that are worshipped, that particular stone is said to bring down heavenly powers. In other words, it holds the keys to the Kingdom of Heaven. And in a euphonious play on words of the type of which mystics are so fond, the Mithrans refer to their peter stone, and their Peter god, as Pater Patrum, 'the father of fathers.' The Mithran high priest is also referred to as Pater Patrum, and he is also referred to simply as Papa. He wears a tall crown in the oblong shape of the sacred peter stone. Now rumor has it that the battle is on, the battle is really on, so that all of the lore and paraphernalia of this ancient place of power under the Vatican are being taken over by the Christians."

Wondered Theophilus, "Or, conversely, are the Mithrans taking over the Christians? Mithraism is the soldiers' religion. It's full of militancy, whereas Jesus was gentle. It's full of secrecy, whereas Jesus was the most open of men."

Said Floralia, "Well, I've told as much as I know of the story. We may or may not live to see the story's upshot."

Then they were both silent. The opium that they had been consuming had a reputation for inducing hallucinations. Both of them were viewing, in their mind's eye, dark goings-on in the Vatican, more clearly than they wanted to.

Then they were both silent. And both sensed something malevolent and foreboding in the air.

Floralia astounded Theophilus by speaking the words that had been about to enter his tongue. "Can that accursed Vatican Peter-stone really reach us here?"

Then all at once they both lunged for the feel of something feminine. They emerged from the bath and began to oil the two oilers. They caressed the two beautiful slave girls North and South, all up and down.

These young ladies were soon writhing with excitement on many of the cushions with which Floralia's premises were amply provided. Covered with expensive perfumed oils, they giggled at the treat of being slathered with the stuff and slathering it on each other.

Floralia mumbled something about wanting to be the guiding hand of Peter. Theophilus could not understand what she said, and could not tell whether it was a jest or a profundity. But it did not matter. He experienced the joy of having Floralia guide his tumescent wine-happy phallus into North and South, each in turn, as they bent over to display their lovely, glossy, well-oiled posteriors. He pleasured the groaning ladies long and with relish. At intervals Floralia took Theophilus' penis in hand, and elsewhere, and enjoyed it while repeating her favorite designation for it in Latin.

"Mmm, *fascinum!*" The organ was fascinum, *the spellbinder*, the source of endless fascination for her, and the very source of the word *fascination* as well. Much time passed in erotic sport, and eventually Floralia had to content herself with varieties of artistic play with whatever little vigor was left in his exhausted *fascinum*. She did not mind at all, this play being for her a dessert after a day of sumptuous banquet.

And on this night, it felt right to sleep with Floralia. The two would find that they were visited by similar dreams this night. They shared weird dreams of the weird god Pater Liber, who could be terrifying but who was also identical with the wonderful god of mystic abandonment and wine: Dionysus, *the god below*.

XV BEFRIENDING THE PRINCE

*L*ife was sweet for Rome's gentlemen of leisure. Days were spent at marketplaces, hairdressers, booksellers, baths, libraries and lectures. Lush banquets and expensive courtesans graced the evenings. Theophilus' months in Rome had passed pleasantly. The return of warm weather now moved many an evening's festivities out into the host's gardens. Hobnobbing in the best circles, as Theophilus now did, was by no means as invariably interesting as he had been led to expect. Bores abounded. But one evening in a garden he was honestly pleased to see a certain familiar face approaching.

"Pliny!"

"Well, good evening good Argonaut Theophilus! And how soon will we be bidding you farewell on your scholar's Odyssey?"

"Quite soon. Unless our last-minute travel preparations turn out to be more time-consuming than expected."

Pliny flicked a hand. "Oh, then you'll be off in no time at all! Travel has never been easier than it is these days: excellent roads, no wars, no borders, no pirates, not too many highway robbers. Everybody's traveling! How many of you will there be in your group?"

"Cato and I will each be taking only one slave."

"Yes, well there's really no need for more. Nowadays one slave is all a gentleman needs to make his travel arrangements. You have no reason to have to dazzle the natives with a retinue!" Pliny paused. "By the way, it has come to my attention that no one ever bothered to inform you that Hadrian definitely won't be accompanying you after all. The succession is a touchy matter, and it just wouldn't do for the likely heir to be away on a long trip in an unofficial capacity. From what I've heard, it would seem that a bit of an intrigue took place. Trajan appeared to be somewhat eager to have Hadrian out of the way for a time, for whatever reason, perhaps a little simple envy. But Empress Plotina, Hadrian's aunt, squelched the travel plan. She's dead set on making quite sure that Hadrian is the heir!"

"I'm very sorry Hadrian won't be able to accompany us," said Theophilus with a straight face.

"Yes, it appears that travel is out. Hadrian is likely to be in for some pretty rigorous training if he is going to be the heir. Trajan is getting down to serious planning of military campaigns in the east, some of the largest campaigns that the legions have ever undertaken. Challenging the Persians themselves! We may live to see Rome's last enemies conquered and all the world brought under Roman rule!"

"If anyone could do that, it seems as though Trajan could. He has a cooler temperament than Alexander. As well as vastly more resources to work with. And presumably vastly more time. But the world is large."

"The miracle may well happen: everywhere Roman roads, Roman laws, Roman peace. I dare to think we're on the threshold of the golden age of human progress. That is, if certain failings in Rome's ruling strata can be rectified. By now, Augustus has been proved to be so right on so many things."

Mentions of Augustus tended to be a trite code denoting a call for a return to traditional values. Theophilus suspected Pliny of coyly alluding to Augustus' long campaign against the many upper class men who remained unmarried and childless. He was almost immediately proved right. As in a play, a goddess suddenly appeared to determine the course of the plot. Pliny introduced Theophilus to his beautiful young niece Marcellina, as had obviously been his intention all along. Eligible upper-class bachelors and maidens could meet only in rare circumstances in semi-formal surroundings, and one such encounter had just been deftly arranged.

Theophilus recited a poem about flowers in a garden and inserted Marcellina's name among the flowers. He instantly regretted having been so banal, but Marcellina beamed. Theophilus was heartened to proceed to enumerate the flowers that came to mind on account of her chestnut hair, her blue eyes, her rosy complexion. Marcellina beamed some more.

Pliny looked very pleased himself. "Theophilus is planning a journey to the east," he said.

Theophilus was drinking in the aura of this stunning young woman, this central attraction of a spring garden. Blooming like spring itself, young Marcellina was probably making her very first appearance in society.

"The east must be lovely," she said. "Silk comes from there. Are you going to where the silk comes from?"

Theophilus now had to come to terms with reality. Marcellina was somewhat lacking in her education.

Yet however poorly she may have comprehended the incredible distance of the Land of Silk she certainly did justice to her gown of silk. It clung to her figure so deliciously that Theophilus was at pains to limit his staring. Not to be able to embrace her then and there was an agony. There was danger there, even more danger than with the letter of Pilate he had craved. A dalliance was out of the question. And anything more than that would spell an indefinite postponement to the all-important journey.

"You'll have to be so careful: my mother says Greeks are all dishonest and they never keep their houses clean!" Marcellina was prattling on. Theophilus' ears were as benumbed as his eyes were bedazzled.

How lucky it was that her conversation was unengaging. And how sad. Theophilus wondered why so many people considered women incapable of mental cultivation. Marcellina did not seem innately unintelligent. She stated that she knew how to read but never bothered to do so. She played a role, as did most everyone. *Such a waste*, thought Theophilus. Yet all might not be lost: she was very young, and alluring despite everything. More than likely, she would hurry his step just a bit on the journey back to Rome after his research had been accomplished.

Soon the guests' bodily subtleties were indicating that a new center of attention had appeared in the garden. By and by, that individual became visible amid his crush of admirers. Astonishingly, he sought out Theophilus.

"This is one man I envy," announced Hadrian. "And that's a bad emotion for a philosopher!"

Theophilus could not imagine how Hadrian's entourage knew that they were supposed to withdraw and leave the two of them alone but withdraw they did. The *Greekling* smelled of too much perfumed lotion. Theophilus wished he would not sit so close.

"I believe I owe you an apology, Theophilus. We shouldn't have left you wondering all this time whether or not I was still interested in accompanying you. I very much wanted to, and my uncle thought the trip would be an invaluable experience, but Aunt Plotina was dead set against it."

The emperor's nephew was being amazingly humble and more amazingly frank. It occurred to Theophilus for the first time that this must be one very lonely young man. He seemed to need a friend.

"Aunt Plotina will wear you down the way dripping water wears down a stone, in order to get what she wants. My uncle thought that my seeing more of the Empire would be a priceless education, but Aunt Plotina would have none of it. She wants me present at the court, and no question about it. To her, anything that jeopardizes my chances to be the heir is most definitely out of the question."

That the exalted stranger Hadrian would so take Theophilus into his confidence astounded Theophilus, and disturbed him more than a little. Not very long ago hearing such revelations could have been dangerous. Also a surprise were the day's revelations about the never-seen Empress Plotina. It would seem that women were not invariably the weak nonentities that they were often assumed to be.

"Certainly, it's disappointing, Dominus," said Theophilus, "but I'm sure you'll have your chance to tour the Empire. I understand you're not even as old as I am."

"Please call me Hadrian. It's a pity we weren't able to travel together, but we can be friends nonetheless."

"Yes, of course, Hadrian. If you like, I can send you letters on my journey."

"I'd like that. And you can write me informally, not the way you'll be sending reports to my uncle. And I understand you write poetry. By all means send me your creations. Every poet is glad of an audience. I know I am! Though I'm not so sure my creations deserve one."

Theophilus wondered if he had misjudged Hadrian. Everything he had said today characterized him as perfectly agreeable. What he said next made him seem more so.

"I hope you'll be someone who'll be helping me in the future, Theophilus. Our generation has opportunities that no other has had. Painful lessons have been learned by the generations before us.

Now in order for there to be a cultural and material flowering such as the world has never seen, all we need is to heed those lessons. I think the end of misgovernment is truly at hand. The end of war may not be far off either."

"I understand that the emperor is planning military campaigns that could end the very existence of multiple states."

"Yes, truly a military man's solution! But the world is bigger than military men know. Where can all the conquering lead? I think the time is ripe to fix permanent defensible boundaries. Don't misunderstand, though. I regard Uncle Trajan as a wonderful man, the best man there is! Character is still built in Spain, while in Italy it's regarded as a joke. But his is a military frame of mind. Not irreparably so, of course. It was his own idea to set up a fund for indigent children; nobody else suggested that. Likewise with planning the construction of the greatest of libraries. I'd like to go even farther and give Rome an academy like Athens' academy. I believe education should begin to be a state concern. Yes, we've quite a lot to do. We're the generation to do it, Theophilus!"

"True, but I'm afraid I'll have to be content with contributing one lone book to Trajan's library for a start," commented Theophilus.

"That's no small thing! No. We must get to the heart of this matter of Christianity. Persecution is not the answer. No. I'm in agreement with my uncle that Christians should not be hounded or even sought. We've got to expose fantastic superstitions for what they are, and give people a reason to resist clinging to them. True religion has got to be revived. For all we know, there may even be a place for this Jesus Christ in legitimate religion. Find this out for us, Theophilus. And write often. I still want to be as much a part of this trip as I can."

This day had been a strange one. Theophilus suddenly had two people that he was sorry to be leaving behind in Rome.

XVI BEGINNING THE JOURNEY

Bright sunlight announced that Theophilus' departure time was near. The sunlight glared against the white plaster placards where Secundus listed the new arrivals at his bookstore. Theophilus scanned these carefully, as always.

"Say, I thought you were keen on the oldest books!" Secundus had come out for some sun. "Come on in, I've got just the thing for you."

Inside, Theophilus had to wait for his eyes to adjust to the darkness before he could read the titulus on the scroll that Secundus set before him. "The *Gospel of John,*" he read. "It's old, you say?"

"In the sense that I've never seen it before this month, it's new. And this particular copy is certainly new. From much of what I saw when I glanced through it, though, I'd say it's actually old. Sometimes you can hardly even judge a book's age by its language. This book is *old-new*. It's written in a slightly pompous style you might call *timeless*. Here, I've rolled it to the beginning for you. See for yourself."

Theophilus read from the manuscript. "*In the beginning was the Word, and the Word was with God, and the Word was God. All things were made through him, and without him was not anything made that was made... The true life that enlightens every man was coming into the world, and the world was made through him, yet the world knew him not. He came to his own home, and his own people received him not. But to all who received him, who believed in his name, he gave the power to become children of God."*

"A captivating enough start," judged Theophilus.

"Yes, it's well written. A very fine Greek. So many of the Gnostic works are really just trash, but I thought you'd be interested in this particular one. It's unique. I've heard the three most popular gospels, *Matthew* and *Mark* and *Luke*, referred to as the 'synoptics' because they see things from basically the same point of view. This gospel has a totally different point of view. If you want it, though, I'll have to ask double the usual price, as it's something of a rarity. So that would be twenty denarii."

Theophilus handed Secundus the coins, twenty little silver coins that represented twenty days of a skilled workman's wages and took the *John* under his arm. He told Secundus, "*John* will have to wait till I'm on my trip before I take a good look at him. That way I'll have something to look forward to."

"Are you leaving so soon then?"

"Yes, very soon. I'll just tuck *John* away in the box of books I'm bringing along."

"You're going to bring a box of books?"

"Yes."

"Books are so expensive and so cumbersome. It seems to me they're awfully likely to be lost or stolen. But that's good for business, isn't it? Perhaps you can suggest to everyone you meet on the road to do the same!"

Soon came the time for Theophilus and his books to be on the road, trundling down the Appian Way along with Cato and their two slaves in a hired carriage. Carriages stood ready for hire at the entrance of nearly every city. They were fine for the baggage and were often fitted out for sleeping because in so many places the inns were rather bad, but when Theophilus traveled he usually preferred to walk or ride a horse as his clumsy hired wagon rumbled noisily along. The contact of human rump to wooden frame to wooden wheels to rough paving stones, without any intervening springs, did not make for a great deal of comfort. Besides, to be outside on the open road in springtime was sheer joy.

Theophilus liked to be out in the spring air watching thousands of paving stones disappear, one by one, beneath his feet. Watching the stones was advisable, due to an abundance of horse manure, but there was much to distract one's attention. For instance, the road leading into or out of every city was lined with tombs that were designed expressly to attract the traveler's attention. Busts, statues, inscriptions, and odd architecture, all vied to catch the eye. Like the papyrus rolls in a library, each grave cried out, "Choose me! Don't pass me by! Grant me immortality! Don't let me be forgotten!"

In city after city the roadside tombs awaited. Between cities, peasants and slaves were hard at work in their picturesque but ever-demanding fields. Theophilus felt lucky that his own springtime exercise was so much more interesting. Now here were the graves again. Each was the petrified remnant of a human experience: the proud portrait of a successful businessman here, a heart-rending poem about a deceased child there; families, couples, the well-remembered with flowers, and the long-forgotten in their crumbling last abodes. Some had despaired. "*Non fui, fui, non sum, non curo,*" read an inscription. "I was not, I was, I am not, I care not." Yet even the author of that satirical epitaph probably had cared. Everywhere the driving urge not to completely perish was apparent. It was only human to care.

Only one city lacked roadside tombs. That city was a tomb.

There, thoughts of the human quest for immortality were bound to be the most poignant of all. Theophilus and Cato walked the black pumice stone that entombed Pompeii. Cato had known Pompeii as a living city. His eyes were filled with tears. Mount Vesuvius brooded above them and even spewed smoke as if to emphasize that it was unapologetic for what it had done. At Pompeii, not even housetops were visible above the hardened ash; nothing. Only the blackness remained. Yet the nearby bay of Neapolis was so beautiful and blue. Theophilus believed he had a subject for the first poem he would write for Hadrian. And a copy would go to Marcellina too. For the most part the poem wrote itself, as he walked the Pompeii pumice. He recited it over and over to himself, sing-song. "*Ecce gratum et optatum ver reducit gaudia. Purpuratum floret pratum. Sol serenat omnia. Iamiam cedant tristia! Aestas redit nunc recedit hiemis saevitia.* (See how the spring, so welcome and so longed-for brings back joy. Ah, the fields of purple flowers. The sun shears through all. So now may cares recede! As summer returns, so retreats the winter that was so cruel.)"

He need only go to the inn and write it down and post it before setting sail at Neapolis to cross the Adriatic. He walked off and left Cato alone with his memories.

THERE WILL FOLLOW MYSTERIUM II GREECE

GLOSSARY

Acts Along with a gospel, an epistle and an apocalypse, a book of Acts was one of the four forms of ancient Christian scripture. Within the Acts genre, only Luke's *Book of Acts* remained well-known and canonical.

Apocalypse Also known as a Revelation, this was a Christian scripture describing the end of the world.

Arche The concept of *the origin of all things*.

Aretology A wonder-laden biography in which the hero is half-man and half-god, and often a Son of God whose miraculous birth is announced by angels, and who comes to save the world.

Ark of the Covenant The most important object of veneration in the Old Testament. It was present in Solomon's Temple but not in Herod's Temple of the first century, having disappeared.

Atrium A square foyer beyond the front door of an affluent Roman house. At its center was a square unroofed pool that held rainwater, and all around it were various decorations and cubicles.

Basilica A Roman court of law, a building that in many cities was transformed into a Christian church.

Beast Epithet of abuse for the worst emperors like Caligula and Nero, later extended to a theological meaning.

Biblia Literally, *the books*. Over the centuries this came to refer solely to the books that composed the Bible.

Calends The first day of the month in the ancient Roman calendar.

Capitoline Hill. Etymologically in some way the *head* of Rome (*caput* = head), this hill housed the temple of the chief of the gods, Jupiter.

Carpe Diem Literally, *Seize the day*.

Cathedra Greek for *chair*, something which was so rare in ancient times as to be almost equivalent to a throne. The word gave rise to the word *cathedral* because a cathedral was the seat of a bishop.

Chi-rho The Greek letter *chi*, looking like an X, superimposed on the Greek letter *rho*, looking like a P. Together they made a symbol standing for *chrestos*, which means *excellent*. An obvious next step was for this symbol to become a symbol for Christ. Christ, the anointed one; the Hebrew equivalent was "Messiah." In the New Testament, the gospels usually referenced Jesus, while Paul usually referenced Christ.

Codex Considered a novelty in the first century, a codex was a book in the form of turn-able pages, rather than in the form of a scroll.

Collegia Throughout the Roman Empire, these were associations of all varieties, considered respectable if ancient but disreputable if new. One of the main advantages of membership in one of the *collegia* was an assured burial.

Concha Latin for *seashell* and *female genitals*.

Corpus Delicti Literally, *the body of the crime*.

Cunnus Latin for *female genitals*.

Decans Astrological divisions of the sky into 70 sections. As Jesus' Twelve Apostles may have symbolized the twelve signs of the zodiac, so his 70 disciples may have symbolized the 70 decans.

Dominus Literally, *Lord*, a title applied to the Roman Emperor, and later to many others considered worthy of respect. Eventually it came to mean *the Lord God* within Christianity.

Dynamis Literally, *mighty act*, one way of referring to a miracle.

Epistle Formal Greek word for a letter or message.

Evangelion Public announcement of glad tidings by a government messenger. Precisely this term was the term used for the gospels.

Evangelium Latin equivalent of *evangelion*.

Fasces Origin of the word *Fascism*, a fasces was an axe wrapped in sticks, symbolizing the Roman state's power to beat and execute.

Fascinum Literally, *the spellbinder*, a term for the penis.

Fiscus Judaicus After the Jewish Revolt, this special tax was applied to all Jews in the Roman Empire. It was equivalent to the tithe that had formerly been paid to the Jerusalem Temple.

Fornix Arched alcove frequented by prostitutes.

Gar The controversial inconclusive Greek word that ended the *Gospel of Mark*.

Gnosis Greek for *knowledge*, and by extension a mystical inner knowledge of the divine.

Gnostics Those who claimed to have *gnosis* or were striving to obtain *gnosis*.

Golden House Nero's extravagant palace, mostly demolished after his overthrow.

Imperium The origin of words such as *imperial, emperor,* and *empire*. Originally, *imperium* was a Roman official's temporary power to command legions and issue decrees.

Institutum Neronianum Nero's anti-Christian legislation.

Ioudaioi Greek for *the Jews*.

Jezebel For Jews, the customary name with which to deride a non-Jewish harlot.

Judaizer A gentile who took an interest in Judaism and observed some of its tenets.

Kolobodaktylos Literally, *stump-fingered*, a term known to have been applied to the gospel-writer Mark, for unknown reasons.

Kteis Greek for *clitoris*.

Land of Silk Known in Latin as *Serica*. This was China, about which the Romans knew next to nothing.

Lupa Literally, *she-wolf*, one of the less respectful terms for a prostitute.

Meretrix Literally, *earner*, a relatively respectful term for a prostitute.

Missa A sending of thanks to God, which was the origin of the Roman Catholic Mass.

Mithraism Sometimes called a religion, but actually was more an all-male cult, with all of its ceremonies conducted in secret, in very small and very deep man-made caverns, usually located near military encampments. Mithrans venerated the eastern astrological deity Mithra, *the joiner*.

Moneta Goddess whose temple on the Capitoline Hill was the place where Rome's coins were minted. The origin of the word *money*.

Optimus Literally, *the best*, a laudatory title for Emperor Trajan.

Orans Standard ancient prayer pose, with upturned palms held high up near the shoulders.

Palatine Hill Origin of the word *palace*. This hill overlooking the Circus Maximus and the Forum was the site of the mansions of the very rich during the Republic but was gradually taken over by the vast palace complex of the emperors.

Papa Short alternative title for the Mithran *Pater Patrum*. The Papa, in the Vatican and elsewhere, was a Mithran High Priest who wore a tall crown in the shape of the sacred patriarchal *peter stone*. Papa is *Pope* in Latin and Italian today.

Pater Liber Literally, the *Father of Liberty*, a title of Dionysus, *The God Below*.

Pater Patrum Literally, *Father of Fathers*, apparently a god and a stone and a High Priest, all venerated by the Mithrans in their patriarchal cult, in the Vatican and elsewhere. The sacred stone could also be called a *peter*.

Pax Romana Literally, *the Roman Peace* throughout the known world that was instituted by Emperor Augustus.

Pollex Verso Literally, *turning of the thumb* to determine whether a defeated gladiator would live or die, but in which direction is not known for sure.

Presbyters Elders. The origin of the word *priest*.

Princeps Origin of the word *prince*. With the meaning *leading citizen*, this was one of the euphemistic titles adopted by Augustus, whose name was itself a title of veneration meaning *the august one*.

Quadrans In the gospels, the tiny coin that a widow contributed to the Temple.

Quinquennium The praiseworthy first five years of the reign of Nero.

Quo Vadis Literally, "Where are you going?" What Jesus as the risen Christ asked Peter when he accosted Peter fleeing Rome. The story comes from the non-canonical (apocryphal) *Acts of Peter.*

Rabbi Jewish honorific, literally, *teacher*, that was the manner in which people addressed Jesus. Generally, rabbis were not leaders of a congregation until after the first century.

Relegatio A writ sending an accused into a temporary exile, in a place of his own choosing.

Retiarii Gladiators equipped with nets and tridents.

Saturnalia The ancient Romans' raucous festival to celebrate the return of the sun in December

Scriptuo Continua Ancient Latin or Greek text written in all-capital letters, with no spaces between the words and no punctuation.

Septuagint The Old Testament as translated into ancient Greek in Alexandria, Egypt. Legend maintained that the text was called the *Septuagint* because the translation work was carried out by 70 scholars.

Shofar Ram's horn blown for Jewish ceremonial purposes.

Son of God Term of honor which was applied to many figures in the Old Testament, and which was applied to Jesus, though he never applied it to himself. The earliest application of the term to Jesus occurred in some versions of the *Gospel of Mark*, but it was absent in other versions.

Son of Man Term, of much disputed import, which Jesus applied to himself frequently.

Thracians Gladiators equipped with a sword, shield, and crested helmet.

Titulus A label bearing a book's title, attached to a scroll.

Torah The first five books of the Old Testament, also known as the Pentateuch, considered vastly more important than the other books.

Vates A witch or seer.

Vatican Originally meant *the hill of the witches*, a place of ill repute on the unfavorable side of the Tiber.

Vigiles Rome's rudimentary police force.

BIBLIOGRAPHY

Aries, Philippe. *A History of Private Life: I From Pagan Rome to Byzantium*. First Harvard University Press. 1992.

Armstrong, Karen. *St. Paul: The Apostle We Love to Hate*. Boston: Icons Series. 2015.

Barbiero, Flavio. *The Secret Society of Moses: The Mosaic Bloodline and a Conspiracy Spanning Three Millennia*, Rochester, VT: Inner Traditions. 2010.

Callahan, Tim. *Secret Origins of the Bible*. Altadena, CA: Millennium Press. 2002.

Casson, Lionel. *Everyday Life in Ancient Rome*. Baltimore: John Hopkins University Press. 1998.

Doherty, Earl. *The Jesus Puzzle: Did Christianity Begin with a Mythical Christ?* Ottawa: Canadian Humanist Publications. 1999.

Ehrman, Bart. *How Jesus Became God: The Exaltation of a Jewish Preacher from Galilee*. New York: HarperCollins. 2014.

Ehrman, Bart. *Misquoting Jesus*. San Francisco: Harper. 2005.

Fidler, D., *Jesus Christ, Sun of God.* Quest Books. 1993.

Freke, Timothy and Peter Gandy. *The Jesus Mysteries: Was the "Original Jesus" a Pagan God?* New York: Three Rivers Press. 1999.

Freke, Timothy and Peter Gandy. *The Lost Goddess: The Secret Teachings of the Original Christians*. New York: Three Rivers Press. 2001.

Helms, Randel. *Gospel Fictions*. New York: Prometheus Books. 1988.

LaCarriere, Jacques. *The Gnostics*. Chicago: Peter Owen Publishers. 2014.

Martin, James, John Beck and David Hansen. *A Visual Guide to Gospel Events*. Grand Rapids, MI: Baker Books. 2010.

Murdock, D.M. *Christ in Egypt: The Horus-Jesus Connection*. Seattle: Stellar House Publishing. 2009.

Murdock, D.M. *Who Was Jesus?: Fingerprints of the Christ*. Seattle: Stellar House Publishing. 2007.

O'Donnell, James. *Pagans: The End of Traditional Religion and the Rise of Christianity*. New York: HarperCollins. 2015.

O'Grady, Selina. *And Man Created God: A History of the World at the Time of Jesus*. New York: St. Martin's Press. 2012.

Sean, Martin. *The Gnostics*. New York Oldcastle Books. 2012.

Smith, Morton. *Jesus the Magician*. New York: Barnes and Noble Books. 1978.

Stark, Rodney. *Cities of God: The Real Story of How Christianity Became an Urban Movement and Conquered Rome*. San Francisco: Harper. 2006.

Tabor, James. *Paul and Jesus: How the Apostle Transformed Christianity*. New York Simon and Schuster. 2012.

Walker, Barbara. *The Woman's Encyclopedia of Myths and Secrets*. San Francisco: Harper. 1983.

Walker, Peter. *In the Steps of Saint Paul: An Illustrated Guide to*

Paul's Journeys. Oxford: Lion Books. 2014.

Wells, G.A. *Who Was Jesus?* LaSalle: Open Court Publishing. 1989.

ABOUT THE AUTHOR

Mitchel Fidel has traveled to nearly all parts of the world, experiencing a full immersion in foreign languages and cultures. He was employed at the Multiversity for Personal Development in India, and his teaching experience has ranged from the Defense Department's National Cryptologic School to the Nizhoni School for Global Consciousness in Santa Fe. With writing experience behind him that included Top Secret intelligence analysis for the National Security Agency and developmental work for two Hollywood internet firms, he undertook the Great Puzzle of first century A.D. spirituality, because so much information in that regard had come to light that it was practically begging to be put into the entertaining configuration of a novel. He lives in Tampa, where he surveys an Egyptic scene of palm trees, lotuses, ibises, and alligators, all from a balcony that is visited by falcons. Mitchel Fidel has been to all of the locales that form the backdrop to the Mysterium series and has studied the relevant historical materials not for years but for decades, making him uniquely qualified to carry out such a project. His colorful lifetime travelogue is available on Facebook (Mitchel Fidel 1), and he welcomes discussion of the innately controversial material presented in his books, on Facebook, on the Goodreads author site "Mitchel Fidel", on Twitter @gnostalogue, and on the website mitchelfidel.com. The Mysterium series will continue with *Mysterium II Greece, Mysterium III Asia, Mysterium IV Judea,* and *Mysterium V Egypt and Beyond.*

DISCUSSION GUIDE
for Book Clubs, Journaling,
or Personal Contemplation

1. Nearly all ancient books have disappeared. If you were given a week to peruse an ancient library, plus the services of a translator, what information, what "mysterium," would you investigate?

2. What is the meaning of the name "Theophilus"? Was this name an intriguing hook for the opening of a novel? Who do you suppose the actual Theophilus was?

3. What visual images of first century Rome stand out for you in Mysterium: I Rome? Were there any that did not match your expectations?

4. Were you able to spot any anachronisms, or any items or attitudes that did not seem correct for the time and place?

5. Can you describe the important character who never appears, Paul? His appearance, attitudes, writings, entourage, experiences, and demise?

6. Another important character who never appears is Emperor Augustus. Can you remember the important points at which he is mentioned? Was your opinion of him favorable or otherwise?

7. What did you learn about the nature of the Vatican in ancient times?

8. Can you name some good deeds and some evil deeds that were performed by various Roman emperors? What do you think of Roman imperial government?

9. What was the importance of the fact that the Colosseum was constructed using funds looted from the Temple of Jerusalem. What is your own feeling about each of these buildings?

10. Floralia claimed that Nero's time was a time of novels, and mentioned one novel that was written at this time for Jews, and one novel that was written at this time for Romans.

What do you know about, and think about, the literature of this period?

11. What clues existed that Luke and Paul were in league with Roman "insiders," and that they were endeavoring to make Christianity more palatable to the Roman establishment?

12. Who, in the novel, though not identified as such, was the fourth pope? What was the nature of his character and his teachings?

13. What is a codex and what are its advantages over a scroll? How was the world different when a major published work would be available in fifty copies? How has printing changed the world?

14. What shortcomings did many people see in the *Book of Mark*? What was his unflattering nickname? What evidence is there that he was unfamiliar with Judea?

15. What made Theophilus dislike Hadrian at first, and what made him change his mind? Did he seem to you to be a positive figure? Do you know what ultimately happened to him?

16. Pater Patrum, alias Papa, and his "peter stone," formed the beginnings of what institution? Does this scenario that is claimed by the novel seem convincing?

17. What are the major differences between the four New Testament gospels described in Mysterium:I Rome?

18. Compare and contrast the people of first century Rome with your contemporaries and peers.

19. Rank in order of importance three facts presented in this book. Rank and discuss the validity of three of the theories presented in the book.

20. What things which were commonly done during the first century in Rome are now considered offensive, barbaric, cruel, or immoral?

21. If you lived in the first century in Rome, what would a normal day be like? Expand on this: Discuss where you would fit in, in society. What might your life expectancy

be? What politics would you espouse? What religion would you follow?

22. What are your spiritual beliefs? How do they compare to the spiritual beliefs of early Christians as portrayed in this book?

23. Describe the three main characters in this book What else do you like to know about them?

24. What do you believe Theophilus will discover during his later journeying, to Greece, Asia, and Judea?

We are an exclusive publishing house.

Our readers, once they finish one of our books, will be able to get up and face the world wiser, stronger, centered, and with the assurance that we are not alone: we are all a part of the Sheltering Tree on Earth.

If you as a writer feel that same calling, please refer to

ShelteringTree.Earth/writer-guidelines